MERK'S MISTAKE

Heroes for Hire, Book 3

Dale Mayer

Books in This Series:

Levi's Legend: Heroes for Hire, Book 1

Stone's Surrender: Heroes for Hire, Book 2

Merk's Mistake: Heroes for Hire, Book 3

Rhodes' Reward: Heroes for Hire, Book 4

Flynn's Firecracker: Heroes for Hire, Book 5

Logan's Light: Heroes for Hire, Book 6

Harrison's Heart: Heroes for Hire, Book 7

Jarrod's Jewel: Heroes for Hire, Book 8

Books in the SEALs of Honor Series:

MERK'S MISTAKE: HEROES FOR HIRE, BOOK 3
Dale Mayer
Valley Publishing

Copyright © 2017

ISBN-13: 978-1-773360-25-6
Print Edition

Back Cover

Welcome to *Merk's Mistake*, book 3 in Heroes for Hire reconnecting readers with the unforgettable men from SEALs of Honor in a new series of action packed, page turning romantic suspense that fans have come to expect from USA TODAY Bestselling author Dale Mayer.

Time never fades…

After months of recovery, Merk is moving from mission to mission, happily back in his active life again. But when his ex-wife sends out a panicked call for help, he rushes to meet her – only to see her snatched away in front of him.

Katina has only one person in mind when she finds herself in trouble. Merk. They haven't spoken for ten years, but time hasn't changed some things. The attraction between she and Merk is as deep and strong as it was back then. Even more so. But with her life on the line, she can't focus on him… and can't get her mind of him.

She has something others want, and they will do anything to get it back. No matter how nefarious. No matter how evil. No matter who they kill.

Sign up to be notified of all Dale's releases here!

http://dalemayer.com/category/blog/

COMPLIMENTARY DOWNLOAD

DOWNLOAD a **_complimentary_** copy of TUESDAY'S CHILD? Just tell me where to send it!

http://dalemayer.com/starterlibrarytc/

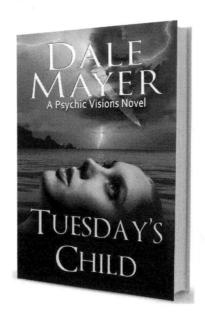

Chapter 1

"THIS IS IT, girl," she said to herself. With a last look around, Katina Marshal took a deep breath and slipped into her car. She jammed the keys into the ignition and started the engine. Wanting her actions to look as normal as possible, she pulled into traffic at a sedate pace and stayed in her lane. She couldn't help studying the rearview mirror to see if she was followed.

Ever since she'd seen the damning information, she'd been planning this for days, subconsciously for weeks, if not longer. Now that it was upon her, her palms sweated profusely, and her heart slammed against her chest.

Everything rode on this escape.

Her gaze darted to the mirror on the passenger side, a frown forming on her forehead as she watched a black car switching lanes to tuck up behind her. Shit. She studied the driver's features, but couldn't see him clear enough. Her breath whooshed out; then, in a sudden move, she shifted to the left lane and slowed. A car honked behind her, but she ignored it.

The car shot past her. With a sigh of relief she picked up speed and blended into the traffic. She had no final destination in mind, just heading west. Away from Houston, from her best friend. Leaving Anna was the hardest thing to do. Katina wasn't tied to her old home or the city, but Anna…

well, Katina also didn't dare put her in danger by stopping to say good-bye.

If only she'd connected with Merk. She'd called him several times but so far, got no answer. She laughed bitterly. "As if he'd help."

Katina knew it was foolish to think of him in that light, but it was hard not to. He held a special place in her heart, plus, he'd been heading for special military training after leaving her. Maybe, just maybe, he'd know how to handle trouble. Like *big* trouble.

And maybe she was just an idiot.

Better to hit the highway and keep running. The people after her would give up soon enough.

Wouldn't they?

Unable to help herself, she reached for her phone and called Merk once more.

Please let him answer.

TWO DAYS TRAVELING to safely deliver one prisoner to Washington and then a shorter trip home, Merk Armand had had enough of airports for the moment. The last trip hadn't been bad, just not short enough. He'd been ready to come home days ago. He located his truck in long-term parking, unlocked the door, and hopped in, instinctively reaching for his cell phone still in the glove box where he'd left it. Found four messages, but didn't recognize the number.

All from the same person. Someone he'd thought to never hear from again.

And his ex-wife, Katina. He was surprised to hear her voice. He called the number but got no answer.

"Damn it." He was too tired for this, but worry niggled at him. He called an hour later when he hit his bedroom. Again no answer.

First thing in the morning he called once more. Still nothing. Worried now, he looked up her number in his cell phone and tried that one. Out of service. So much for that idea. Determined to put her calls out of his mind, he walked toward the garage door, heading into town for supplies. A full day of errand running. Oh, joy. But it was necessary. The men were doing upgrades on the compound, and having just got back, Merk was the one with the most flexible time to handle this.

Just as he stepped into the garage, his cell phone rang. He pulled it out. Katina again. He quickly answered it. "Hello? Katina?"

Only a strange static answered him. Damn it. He disconnected, then quickly hit Redial. No answer. Frowning, he turned back to the group working in the garage, their R&D room, and said, "I've got the list but don't expect me back anytime soon after you and Ice added half a dozen more things to my day."

Merk walked to the truck, one of several company vehicles that Levi had picked up. The company Levi had created with Ice was doing extremely well. But it also meant they had teams moving in and out all across the country, depending on what their current projects were. Sometimes it was simple security detail, like Logan's job in California right now, leading a team of bodyguards for a big-name singer.

Merk gave a shudder at that thought. Not that he couldn't do the job; it just wouldn't be his first choice. He was a people person in small groups, not large crowds like that. And when he led a security detail, he wanted free rein to do what was necessary. Not maximum force, but some. And Logan's hands would be more or less tied.

Although being in California right now would not be a good idea. Merk needed to figure out these weird calls from his ex-wife. Not that the term *wife* actually applied here. They'd known each other for only a few hours when they decided marriage was a great idea. Part of the reason for hooking up in the beginning was they were both from Houston, and it had blown up from there. But then what did he expect of a wild party weekend in Vegas? He wasn't ashamed of it, but neither was he proud. One of those chapters of his life he'd like to call closed.

He'd been young and stupid. His last fling before he headed into BUD/S training. A bunch of them had gone down to Vegas for the week, and he'd fallen in lust and celebrated by getting thoroughly drunk. The cold hard reality had hit them both in the morning around the same time as their hangovers.

Only years later did he realize he'd been dating other women who looked exactly like her. Katina had been small with long blonde hair—not plain, not gorgeous, but when she smiled, her whole face lit up. And he'd been instantly enthralled. Enough that he'd bought a marriage license right then and there. Sure the margaritas might have had something to do with that—at least with them following through on it. Tequila was always a shit drink for him, allowing him to indulge without showing signs, then knocking him silly when he hit the worm at the bottom. They had one hell of a night and had both woken up the next morning in shock and horror.

It was almost funny, laughable really, at how quickly they'd gotten dressed, sat down over coffee, and figured out how they'd undo the mess. When they finished the research, grabbed the paperwork, and filled it out, they still had to wait one year to file for the no-contest divorce. But they'd done what they could at the time. He'd left for his training the same day.

In a way that got him through the horrible nightmare of training too. Nothing like seeing yourself as the fool you really are and knowing you need to change. It had helped him to dig within, make it through some of the deepest, darkest times to find himself. He'd been a different man ever since. And he had never heard from Katina after the filing.

Until now. He had no idea why she was calling. Getting out of the compound for the day would be perfect.

He waited for Stone to move his truck, but he stood in the doorway talking to Ice and Levi. Stone was moving his new girlfriend, Lissa, into the compound. Lissa was a dear. And she'd been to hell and back. Merk had had a hand in her rescue in Afghanistan, but as it sometimes did, the war had followed them home. Her place had been thoroughly trashed, though it was all good now. Between the insurance estimates and the work getting done, they'd spent a lot of days traveling back and forth to her townhome.

But today was their move-in day to a new apartment for them in the compound. As Merk watched Stone hop into the truck and drive away, Merk muttered, "Jesus, has it only been six weeks since we met her? Seems like we've known her forever."

He pulled out of the compound, hit the gas as he reached the main road, and sped toward Houston. He laughed as he passed the small town only minutes from home—and the scene of a pretty dramatic incident of late. All in all, Levi and the new company had had a baptism by fire. Merk reached over and hit the radio button to see what music he could drum up down here. It was country, and he was just not into that sad twang.

After the divorce, he'd stuck to very simple relationships. One big mistake in his life was enough. Seeing Ice and Levi finally work through their shit and become that perfect couple would've been nauseating if they didn't have everybody else wanting the same thing for themselves too. Ice and Levi were devoted to each other.

And now there was Stone, finally surrendering from his hard stance of nothing long-term, only amplified after losing his leg. He'd fallen hard for Lissa.

Merk felt like the two women had turned their matchmaking gazes on everybody else in the compound. And Merk just shook his head, his hands raised in protest, saying, "Don't look at me. Don't look at me."

Merk drove up the ramp and hit the main freeway. It was a nice drive, and he liked being on the open road. Twenty minutes from the city, his phone rang. He had forgotten to hook it up on the dash. He quickly placed it on the holder so he could talk hands-free and said, "Hello." In the background was a weird crackling noise. And more static. He repeated, "Hello, who's this?"

Then came a voice that, although he hadn't heard it in ten years, was impossible to mistake. "Merk, it's me. Katina."

"Hey, I've been calling you." He grinned. "What the hell are you doing contacting me after all this time? Are the divorce papers wrong or something?"

He wished he could take those words back. It had been a joke of a marriage. Wouldn't it be stupid if the divorce were too?

"No, nothing like that," she said hurriedly. "I'm in trouble."

He frowned. "What kind?"

What he knew or remembered of Katina was just a college girl in Vegas for a fun weekend. She'd knocked him flat right at the beginning. But she wasn't the kind of girl to get into trouble.

"I need your help, please."

"If I can," he said cautiously. "What's this all about?"

"I'm in Houston right now. I need to talk with you."

"I'm almost fifteen minutes out. I can meet you for lunch if you want."

Inside he was wondering what the hell he was doing. She might be a slice of his past, but a door he probably should keep closed.

"Joe's Bar and Grill on Main Street. You know it?" she said as her voice rose in a panic, rushed as if she was afraid she'd run out of time before he agreed.

"No, but I can find it." He entered the city limits, hating the traffic pulling up on all sides of him. He vaguely knew where Main Street was, but it was still an hour away from lunchtime.

"Meet me at noon." And she hung up.

Worried, curious, and frustrated. Yeah, that was about the state of affairs in his head. It gave him less than an hour to get a couple stops out of the way and then head there for lunch. He hadn't even planned on stopping for food, but obviously his day was shot to shit already, so what the hell.

By the time he pulled up to Joe's Bar and Grill and parked in the back, he was running ten minutes behind. He'd call her to let her know he would be late but got no answer. And no voice mail. He walked into the smoky bar in a shady part of town, wondering what the hell she was doing down here.

The clean, wholesome college girl hoping to celebrate her twenty-first birthday in style that he remembered would never be caught dead in a place like this.

Then he had to stop himself. Hell, they had been in an Elvis Presley Wedding Chapel together. So maybe this wasn't as far off as he thought. He took a seat by a window and ordered a beer. There had to be something good to this day, so he'd take it now in liquid form.

He didn't allow himself to drink very much. They always had to be ready to head out on the next mission. And being bright-eyed, bushy-tailed, and with all their mental faculties and physical prowess intact meant not letting themselves get shit-faced. Besides, Vegas was always in the back of his mind.

Merk waited ten minutes, slowly sipping his drink, wondering what the hell was going on. But he saw no sign of her. He could see the traffic on Main Street, but not the back of the building, and instinct told him he needed to switch sides. What if she was out back waiting, not wanting to come in? If she was in trouble, it complicated all kinds of things.

He ordered a coffee and told the bartender to deliver it to the other side of the bar. Casually, trying not to draw attention to himself, he sat where he could stare out at the parking lot. No one was there. Thinking he'd been stood up, he finished his coffee and got to his feet. If she needed help, it was either too damn late or she'd had had second thoughts.

The too-damn-late part was worrisome, because it could mean her trouble had found her a whole lot faster than she'd expected. He walked back outside and stood next to the doorway.

"I don't have time for this shit. My day is full already."
He headed around back to the parking lot when he thought
he saw her standing by a small red car.

His footsteps slowed as he studied her. Size and shape
was about right, but he hadn't seen her in eleven years and
she wasn't facing him. She was also too far away to get a
really good look. Determined to get to the bottom of this, if
one was to be found, he walked toward her. She looked
around fearfully, and he realized maybe she hadn't expected
him to go inside the building and had been waiting in the
parking lot for him. She took one look at him and bolted.

"Katina?"

She came to a stuttering stop, turned, and called out,
"Merk?"

Her voice said she hadn't recognized him any easier than
he had her. He nodded. Relief washed over her face, and she
ran back toward him.

A van raced into the parking lot between them and
stopped. Two men got out, grabbed Katina, and threw her
inside. He barely had time to register what had happened
before the van drove right past him. He tried to jump on
board, but the vehicle was moving too fast. As he went down
and rolled, trying to catch sight of the license plate, he
realized there wasn't one.

He was in his truck, the engine roaring, and out of the
parking lot in a flash. He knew all too well how easy it was to
kidnap women and how absolutely impossible to find them
most of the time.

Chapter 2

S HE WAS SUCH a fool.

Why had she run away from him? But he was big, and his hair was cropped short, and she had barely recognized him. Hell, even now she wasn't sure it was him. For all she knew, a complete stranger had nodded at her, thinking she was talking to him. But he'd called her name. It had to have been him. Only, instead of running toward him, she'd run away. Now look what the hell happened. Her one chance of freedom was gone. She'd been flung into the back of a van, a hood quickly pulled over her head, and then tied up.

She hadn't even caught a decent glimpse of the two men who had grabbed her. The vehicle moved in a crazy, erratic pattern that rolled her from side to side. Someone booted her hard, making her roll over the other way. It was all she could do to stifle her sobs.

She'd been threatened, told to stop, and to hand over what she'd taken. But none of the choices had been much of an option.

Where was she supposed to go now? These people had long arms and a lot of resources. And for their crimes, they wouldn't stop until they tossed her lifeless body into a river. Or worse, put cement shoes on her and dropped her in the ocean alive. She was pretty sure it had happened to a few other people who had crossed their path. Only she had no proof. How the hell could she get out of this?

She didn't cry often, and she sure as hell wouldn't now. She was too damn mad. At herself, at Merk.

Why the hell hadn't he been there earlier? Then she realized he had come from around the building. As if toward his vehicle with his keys in his hands. Had he been waiting for her in front? Or even inside? Had she told him to wait outside or inside? She no longer remembered.

She wasn't acting or thinking clearly anymore. Panic had overtaken her world. And now she could barely breathe.

The vehicle took a hard left, and she was flung to the side once more. She slammed her back into something again. She couldn't hold back the moan.

"Stupid bitch, stay where you are."

How the hell was she supposed to do that when they were driving like crazy men? Why *were* they driving like that? It would bring attention to them. She stifled back a gasp of hope. Unless they already had unwanted attention. Was it possible Merk had given chase? Was he even now calling for help? Please let him be calling the police. It was the only way she would get out of this mess. She should have done that first, but was afraid the men after her had connections high up in law enforcement. She didn't know who to trust.

So she had called Merk. His had been the first to come to her mind when she realized she was in deep trouble. Maybe, just maybe, he had become a SEAL—one of the few goals he'd shared with her in his drunken haze. She understood the stats that almost nobody made it through the training, and she really didn't know who he was personally. But she'd hoped … Damn, she'd hoped he'd be here for her.

She closed her eyes and forced herself to breathe as naturally as she could. With the hood over her head it was hard, but she didn't want to hyperventilate, and she could feel the dizziness starting. And then the din around her set in.

"Lose the bastard."

"I'm trying to. What do you think I've been doing for the last ten minutes?"

"Farting around. Get rid of him."

Another voice kicked in. "And if you can't, pull over and let me drive. I'll shake this asshole."

She smiled. So maybe calling Merk hadn't been the biggest mistake she'd ever made. It is possible she would get lucky and somebody would help her—for once.

The vehicle turned yet another corner, tires squealing, men swearing, and then came music to her ears—sirens. And now they were really cussing.

"Move it, move it."

"Fuck that shit. We can't have the cops coming down on us. Get the hell out of here."

"I am. Just give me a minute. I can get to the tunnels and lose them there."

"You can't go in there the wrong way, damn it. Oh, shit!"

Instead of shouting, there was silence. But the vehicle hurtled at top speed, and she realized they would likely end up in a major crash. And if she wasn't lucky, she would die in this damn tin box. She'd be okay if they all did, only she wasn't up for going under at this point in time.

Still, she was incapable of doing anything about it. She was trying, but her feet were bound and her hands tied up behind her with some heavy rope, though the knots around her feet were unraveling with all her rolling around. Then came more shouting.

"Watch out."

"Holy shit, that was close."

The vehicle swerved and wavered as the sirens behind them grew nearer, louder. She had no idea where the hell Merk was in all this. She didn't want him to get in trouble, or hurt, but she sure hoped he hadn't left her.

The sirens were a huge sign. Only the vehicle's momentum never stopped. It was a Monday, and she knew the traffic had been heavy before they put the bag over her head. This *was* Houston. But the van still zigzagged through vehicles while pulling off this escape. In her world of darkness she could hear metal crunch against metal as cars slammed together, punctuated by screaming brakes, then impact sounds. Suddenly, they were out of the darkness and back into daylight. Even with the hood over her head she could sense the difference in the light around her.

"Take a left. The auction yard is just ahead."

The van turned that way, follow by a hard right, then the driver hit the brakes so fast she was flung forward. She slammed into something sharp. She cried out in pain. Her leg, shit, it was injured. Hopefully not bad enough to stop her from running because if she got a chance, she was out of here. She lay on the floor, gasping for breath. Grateful they had stopped that suicidal run, at the same time her ears were alert, searching for the sirens.

But found only silence. Her shoulders sagged as she realized they'd actually done the impossible. They'd escaped. From the police and Merk, she was still a captive. The door opened, and she was grabbed, tossed to the ground outside. She cried out as she landed, her injured leg slamming onto the hard dirt.

"What you want to do with her?"

"Keep her with us. We need new wheels. Pick out something from the lot and hotwire it. We'll throw her in the back again."

And that's when she realized she could see ever-so-slightly through the hood they'd placed over her head. Some burlap sack. Like so much of the shit made today, lacking textile quality. The holes were wider than normal. She watched the men spread out, she counted four, looking for another set of wheels.

She was in a used car lot or junkyard. Vehicles were everywhere. What a perfect place to hide the van. At the same time, maybe she could get herself out of here too.

She sat up, kicked the now loosened rope off her legs, hopped to her feet, and turned to look around, anxious to find any place to hide. She darted in between the first row of cars. The men had gone to the left; she went right.

And she just kept on running. Twenty yards later she tripped and fell, hitting the ground hard, her face going into the dirt. She sat up, spitting, but at least the fall had loosened her hands. With her arms free, she quickly took the hood off her head. She could see where she was clearly now. A main road was not far away.

Staying low, ducking between the vehicles, she ran and kept going until she reached a gate. But she couldn't open it. She didn't know how they got into this place, but the wire atop the fence could be electrified.

She kept following along the perimeter, looking for the gate they had come in through. And then she heard one gunshot in the distance. She clapped a hand over her mouth to hold back her cries and slid under a vehicle. If nothing else she could hide. After the weapon had fired, she heard sounds of a car racing up and down the rows. And men shouting.

Followed by blessed silence. She lay under the vehicle, gasping for air, trying not to cry out loud. But the sobs still came out. Where had they gone? And why? Was she safe?

Had they all left? Or was someone still waiting for her?

Sirens came screaming toward the lot. And then all hell broke loose. For sure she knew the men who'd kidnapped her were gone. She didn't know who had been shot, but knew there was a chance that right now she was safe. Or she could get the next bullet.

Within minutes she heard someone calling. "Katina, are you here?"

"Katina?" another man called.

"Katina, where are you? Are you hurt?"

All unfamiliar voices. And she realized they were systematically searching for her. She couldn't see them yet, so she waited. But even if they were policemen, could she trust them? Then she heard a voice that made her heart swell with joy.

"Katina, its Merk. Where the hell are you?"

In the silence that followed, she could almost hear him growling. He was so close.

"I saw the car leave, and you weren't in it, so I know you're here somewhere. Are you hurt? We'll search this place from top to bottom, but if you can hear me, make a sound or let us know where you are."

"Here," she cried out. "Merk, is that you?"

And suddenly there he was, his face just inches away from hers as he crouched down beside the car she was under.

And he grinned. "There you are. Can you get out? Are you hurt?"

She dragged herself along the ground until she was clear of the vehicle, then Merk snatched her up into his arms and turned around, calling out, "She's here."

Carrying her, he walked to a dozen policemen and their vehicles. The men quickly surrounded them. She couldn't stop crying. God, she hated that. In times of stress it was such a relief to cry, but at the same time, it made her look so damn … female.

Merk asked again, "Are you badly hurt?"

She raised her hand to touch his face, whispering, "I think I'm okay. My thigh hurts, but not too bad."

"We have an ambulance coming," one of the policemen said. "Blood's coming from the back of her leg. She should be checked out."

"Do you know where they were taking you?" Merk asked in a hard voice.

She shook her head as her sobs kept erupting. "No," she said. "I have no idea."

"Why did they kidnap you? Did you recognize those men?"

"No," she whispered. Now, she realized, she was safe. "I've never seen them before."

She opened her mouth to tell them more and held back. Her gaze caught sight of a dead man on the ground. She closed her mouth, then whispered, "Was he the driver? I heard the shot but didn't know who'd been hit."

"We're not sure who he was. I was hoping you could tell us," one of the cops said.

Wide eyed, she shook her head. "I had a hood over my head most of the time. I never had a chance to see anyone."

Merk squeezed her against his chest, and she could feel that insistent gaze as he stared down at her. She opened her eyes to see him, then she made a tiny, hardly perceptible, nod to the men around them. Instantly Merk understood.

She had no idea how, but he did.

Thankfully, the ambulance arrived. Merk carried her over.

She gripped Merk's hand tight and whispered, "Please, I don't want to go to the hospital."

"Depends on how bad it is."

"It's not. I'm good." She turned to stare at him, willing him to understand. "I will die in the hospital."

She consented to having the EMTs check her out. As she sat on the edge of the ambulance, the coroner arrived for the dead man. She stared blindly out at the yard; emergency vehicles were everywhere. Over a trailer was a sign. Action Auctions. She shuddered. What a great place to switch out vehicles.

The EMTs did what they could and one said, "She should get checked at the ER."

She hopped to her feet, crying out, "No." She took a few steps experimentally, and although she winced, the pain wasn't bad. "Nothing's broken. I'll go home and see my doctor. If I need painkillers or something, he'll get me the prescription."

The EMTs told her it was her choice. Merk led her back to his big truck, and she smiled. It was as badass as he was. When she went to open the door, his big hand got there first. He opened it, gently lifted her up, and placed her on the passenger seat.

"Stay here."

He closed the door, but just before it shut, she stuck her head out and said, "What will you say to the police?"

He gave her a reassuring look. "That we'll come down and give a statement."

Disappointed, she slumped in her seat. Not what she

had expected. There would be a hell of an investigation over this.

The trouble was, she didn't dare tell any of them the truth.

MERK HAD NO idea what the hell was going on. But she obviously felt other police were, or could be, involved, and she was just as terrified about the hospital. He wasn't sure what to do with her, but she couldn't be left alone right now. He needed to get her away somewhere private to find out what was happening.

After assuring the cops he'd bring her to the police station later this afternoon once he had a chance to calm her down, they let him go. The police had other things to do as well, and she needed to rest a bit. Maybe he'd take her to the doctor first. His plans for the day had completely changed, and mentally he prioritized the rest of it.

The cops grumbled until he handed over his card and said, "Contact Levi if you got a problem with this, but I personally promise she will be there."

"She should still go to the hospital," one of them said. "That cut's pretty deep."

Merk nodded. "She's hoping to see her doctor. I'll get her checked out first, then we'll be in." As he walked away, he said, "If you guys aren't there, who do we report to at the station?"

One of the men stepped forward and said, "I'll open the file on this one." He handed over his ID and said, "Contact me when you arrive. I'll be there in a couple hours. We'll do a thorough search of this place, especially looking for the getaway van, to see if they left anything behind."

"Good enough."

Merk walked back to the truck, happy to see she hadn't left, but noticed she'd slipped down, as if not wanting anybody to see her. He hopped up in the truck, turned on the engine, and slowly reversed out of the auction yard. As far as a hiding place went, this was a damn good spot.

"Wait."

He hit the brakes. "What?"

She pointed. "There. Isn't that the van they kidnapped me in?"

He parked, jumped down, and walked to the vehicle. It blended in with the others perfectly, as if it belonged. He checked the back for a license plate and realized she was right. There wasn't one.

Opening the side door, he took a quick look, then reached for the glove box. No papers anywhere. He quickly wrote down the VIN number and then called the cops over. When the police arrived, he explained this had been the vehicle they'd been chasing down.

The men went to work. When he got into the truck, he turned to her and said, "Anything else?"

She shook her head. "No. Please, can we just get the hell away from here?"

He nodded, and this time when he exited the auction yard, he kept going.

Chapter 3

"**C**AN YOU DRIVE me to my car, please? I really want my wheels back."

She sat curled up in the corner on the far side of his truck. She stared at his profile, wondering how he'd become such a big man. It seemed like the man she had married had almost been a boy compared to who sat beside her now. He was a hell of a lot more attractive and powerful-looking now too. How could that be? Seemed people got worse when you hadn't seen them for a decade or so. Instead he'd gotten seriously better. He was sexy as hell.

She shook her head. Even back then she knew how to pick them.

"When will you tell me what the hell's going on?"

"It's better if I don't say anything," she said hurriedly. "These guys have obviously proven they will do anything they can to shut me up, and I don't want you to get hurt."

His head spun toward her, his glare hard, the glint lethal. "Don't even play that shit game with me. You're in trouble, and I am one of the few people on this goddamn planet who can help you. So just shut the hell up with that kind of talk, and tell me what's going on."

They were almost at the rear of the pub now. "I need to get my car, give a statement, and have my leg looked after," she said. "After all that, if I have any energy left, I'll tell you."

On that note he drove right through the parking lot. "So we'll go to the police first." He glanced over and saw the look on her face. "No, change that. Clinic first to get you treated, the police second, and then back here for your car."

She glared at him. "You didn't used to be so high-handed."

"And you didn't used to be so stupid." He glared at her. "You really think I'd let you run off with these men after you? Like hell."

"This is big," she protested. "Like, really big."

"Good," he snapped. "Because I do big, so just get used to it."

She subsided into silence, wondering how her life had gotten so crazy. But it didn't matter now because he had just pulled up beside a clinic and parked. He got out, but when he slanted a gaze at her, she realized he was still pissed.

She watched as he walked around and opened the passenger door. Although he might be angry, it wasn't directed at her.

He held out a hand and said, "Take it easy getting down."

With his help she got out of the truck. Her first step brought a cry to her lips. She limped forward, murmuring, "Thank you."

But he didn't drop her hand. Instead he led her inside the front door of the building. Thankfully, it wasn't very busy. She had to wonder if she'd won the lottery on that note.

Once inside, she had her leg cleaned, the doctor put a couple stitches in, bandaged it, and she was back outside in less than ninety minutes.

She shook her head. "Was it because of your presence

that we got in and out so fast?" she added with a note of humor.

"Maybe." He shrugged. "I didn't give a shit as long as you were taken care of." He helped her back into the truck and walked to the driver's side.

She watched as he hopped in easily. "Now where?" she asked.

"Police station. Let's get that damn statement down so we can be done with all the necessities."

As much as she wasn't looking forward to it, she knew he was right.

Besides he wasn't giving her much choice.

Finding parking at the police station, now that was a different story. She hadn't quite understood when they got to the clinic why it was so empty. But when they had arrived at the station, she figured it had been because three-quarters of the damn town was here. Merk still somehow pulled off a miracle locating an empty spot in the far corner. Her leg was damn sore though, so the walk wasn't something she appreciated, but this had to get done.

"I'd offer to carry you now, but chances are you wouldn't want that," Merk said at her side.

She shot him a look. "I don't remember you carrying me over the threshold way back when."

He let out a bark of laughter and said, "I wondered if we would bring up that point in our lives." In a move that shocked a squeal from her, he stooped and picked her up, carrying her around to the front of the station. "You're due one trip over the threshold now since I missed an opportunity way back when."

"You were probably too drunk," she said, a smile on her face.

"And, therefore, chances are *you* were too to remember anyway," he reminded her.

And without another word that settled them back down, both knowing where they'd been, what they'd done, and surprised to find themselves in today's situation.

She still wondered at the impulse to call him when she'd been in trouble. But as it turned out, it had been the best decision she'd made in a long time.

Inside, he set her down near the chairs as they had to wait. Finally, the detective came out and took them to his desk. She wrapped her arms around her chest and tried to answer the questions calmly. She wasn't sure she should say very much though, so a few times she hedged, giving only half answers. She'd been warned not to go to the police, so she didn't really understand what she was supposed to do now. Given a choice, she wouldn't have come to give a statement at any time.

She'd been willing to run halfway across the country, and still planned to, if she could get back to her wheels. Her apartment was gone; she'd been living in a hotel for the last few nights, and they'd still found her. They'd even called her cell phone. The policeman's questions kept coming, but she fell into monotone and monosyllabic answers. "I'm sorry. I'm just so tired, and the pain is really kicking in," she whispered.

The police officer looked at her in sympathy. He printed off her statement, then handed it to her for her signature. "There you go. If you can wait a few more minutes, we have to ask your friend some questions," he said. "Then you can both go home."

"Sure," she said with a faint smile.

Her leg throbbed. They'd given her a shot when they

put the stitches in, but it was wearing off. She thought she had a prescription in her pocket because the doctor had handed her a piece of paper, but hadn't looked at it. She'd just shoved it in a crumpled ball into the corner of her jacket pocket. She rarely took drugs, knowing she would be sleepy and therefore too tired to drive if needed. But right now ... she wished she had them.

She listened as Merk gave his answers, then realized he did exactly as she had. He was hedging. Giving half-truths, not exactly lying, but not giving everything. And with that one little act she trusted him all the more.

How stupid was that? But he was covering her ass as well as his, and she appreciated that. When he was finally done and signed his statement, he stood up and reached out a hand for her.

By the time they stood outside, she wasn't sure she could stand much longer—not to mention drive. Besides, her car was a standard.

And for some reason that truth hadn't kicked in until she looked at his truck. She stared at it in dismay. "I don't know if I can drive."

"Doesn't matter because you're not trying."

"I can't just leave it in the parking lot. It'll get towed."

"I've got that figured out."

He half boosted her into the seat and closed the door on her. By the time he got around to his side and hopped in, she was busy asking, "What do you mean by that?"

But he didn't answer. Instead he left the lot and drove back to the pub where her car was parked.

That's when she remembered something else he had said. "I'm sorry for messing up your day."

He grimaced. "I had a full list of errands, but I'm not

too optimistic about getting any of it done."

"I'm so sorry."

He shrugged. "I still have to pick up a bunch of supplies, but the rest may have to wait until tomorrow or the next day." He glanced up and down the street as if sorting out where they were. "We'll deal with those issues once we address your car."

She leaned her head back and wondered what the hell that meant, but she felt just shitty enough not to give a damn until he pulled into the rear of the pub and parked behind her car.

He reached out a hand and said, "Where are the keys?"

She stared at him blankly. "Why do you want them?"

He motioned toward a man standing before them. "This is Levi. He'll drive your car back."

"Back where?"

Merk gave her a hard stare and said, "Back to the compound where I live."

She opened her mouth to protest, then realized she really had no option. She couldn't drive; she was in shitty shape. She really needed somebody to take charge, at least for a few hours. She dug into her pocket and handed over her keys. Then she watched while Merk hopped from the truck to speak to the big man in front of them.

The discussion lasted about ten minutes with various hand movements she couldn't make heads or tails of. Finally, Merk climbed back into the truck and said, "Good. He'll help pick up the supplies I came into town for."

"You're not making any sense. He had to get into town somehow, and if he's driving my car, how is his own getting home?"

Merk laughed. "Lay your head back and go to sleep. If

you were feeling normal, you'd know that answer."

They drove past another big truck almost identical to Merk's. A beautiful blonde was at the wheel. Merk nodded lightly; she waved, and they carried on. Instantly a stab of jealousy fired through Katina. Who the hell was that woman?

MERK DIDN'T HAVE a clue what was going on in Katina's life, but something sure as hell was. He wanted to question her, but she was in no shape right now. Her eyes were fuzzy with pain, her body hunched into the corner, and her arms were across her chest. She should be asleep in a few minutes.

But he had lots of stops to make. He'd split up the load with Levi, but they were running out of time before the businesses closed. Still he would grab what he could, and then he'd return to the compound. He shook his head. Who'd have thought his day would end this way?

He hadn't seen her in eleven years. And out of the blue, she called asking for help.

Well, before she could leave the compound, he would learn a whole lot more about this trouble she was in because he'd seen her get snatched. This was no simple hit. No stranger abduction. She'd been targeted. And he wanted to know why. That they'd shot one of their own men and left him behind told Merk a much bigger issue was going on. Also she didn't speak truthfully to the cops. So either she didn't want them involved or didn't trust them.

Not that Merk didn't either, but he'd been burned and betrayed himself. His whole unit had, so he'd given only minimal information in his statement. It was just as important to understand who your enemy was. And at this point, he had no clue. When he stopped at his third store, he raced inside to pick up the materials for Stone's latest prototype, returned to the truck, and tossed the items behind the seat. He realized she'd finally given up the ghost and had fallen asleep. He stopped and studied her features for a long moment, then reached out a finger and stroked her cheek.

In a low voice he murmured, "I wonder what trouble you've gotten yourself in, Katina. But if you think you can just tease me with little bits and pieces, you're damn wrong. I will get to the bottom of this, with or without your permission." He settled into his seat, buckled up, and turned on the engine.

He'd never backed down from a fight yet. And when those men had kidnapped Katina, he wanted nothing more than to get his hands on them.

Chapter 4

S HE WOKE UP when the truck came to a sudden stop. She sat up, groggy, and stared as they passed through a huge metal gate into a large fenced area with several buildings. Several other trucks were parked outside, just like the one she was in.

She turned toward Merk and said, "Where are we?"

"Hey, how are you feeling?"

"Better," she admitted. "But you're not answering my question." She gazed around and realized another vehicle came up behind them. They parked alongside her car. She turned again with a questioning look at Merk. "Is this the compound you were talking about?"

"Yes, it's where I live and work."

She studied the layout. It was huge. Her gaze went straight back to the man who got out of her car. He was as big as Merk, if not bigger. And stunning. But more than that, he carried himself like Merk. The same air of can-do attitude and controlled power.

From around the building, the blonde goddess walked toward the other man, and with a smile, he wrapped an arm around her shoulders, and they went into the large building together.

Abruptly Katina told Merk, "I want my keys."

"You can have them." Merk opened his truck door,

hopped out, and walked around to open her door. "Let's get you down and then inside." He stepped back slightly to give her a bit of room. "Then I have to unload the truck."

She slid to the ground without his help and winced only a little as her feet slammed to the ground. The pain wasn't too bad. She took a few experimental steps and realized that, although it hurt, it wasn't crippling. "Feels much better," she said to him, already grabbing things from his vehicle. "I can go home on my own now."

"You could, but you have to go inside and ask for your keys back." He turned and walked away from her, his arms full.

"Or you can get them for me," she called, standing beside her car, "and save me some steps."

"If it hurts that much, then you can't drive anyway."

The door to the house slammed behind him. She glared at it. She wasn't walking in there. She didn't know anybody here. She turned and leaned against her car and waited for him to come back out. It took about five minutes, then he arrived whistling.

Nice that he was happy. She asked, "Did you get my keys?"

"I did." He tossed the keys in the air and then while she watched, caught and shoved them into his jeans pocket.

"That's not fair," she protested. "Give me my keys."

"If you think you're driving away with that leg, you're wrong."

She glared at him. "Who died and made you boss?"

He turned and pinned her with a look. "You did the minute you called me for help." He took a step toward her, and in a low voice, said, "Now get used to it. I'm here to help and I'm not walking away. No matter what you say or how you try to push me away."

Shit. Now what the hell would she do?

When he came back out for the third round of goods from the truck, he stopped and said, "You ready to go inside and meet the others now?" She crossed her arms over her chest and said, "And if I don't want to?"

He shrugged. "Well, they're waiting for you, but if you don't want to be social, that's okay. You can stay out here. It'll get mighty cold soon though. Inside it's nice and warm with hot food and coffee." As he walked away again, his arms once again full of the truck's contents, he called back, "We might all be warriors, but we don't bite off innocent heads."

She glared at the door and thought about how helpful he had been otherwise. He was right. She'd called, and he'd come running. He'd saved her life. Going in and socializing for a few moments, well, it was the least she could do.

Fine.

When he came out the next time, she stood almost at the doorway. He stopped when he saw her and smiled. "Glad to see you're being reasonable." He motioned to the truck. She waited until he picked up the remaining boxes and walked toward her. She held the door open for him, and he walked in, unconcerned if she followed or not.

He was making her crazy again. He'd been like that eleven years ago, and they'd only known each other for a day.

She followed him in. He took a left and laid all the boxes in the middle of the room. She turned and looked at the contents in fascination. Like a huge garage but with workbenches and more, as if they did some fancy development work here.

As he walked toward her again, she eyed him carefully and asked, "Just exactly what do you do for a living?"

"Private security," he said simply.

"Oh."

He took her hand and said, "Come on."

He walked with her into what appeared to be a kitchen with a long bench. In the center of the room were at least half a dozen people.

She stood awkwardly beside Merk as the goddess-looking woman turned and saw her. "Hello, my name's Ice. Who are you?"

And the words that flew from her mouth were not what she had ever expected to say. "Merk's wife."

The room froze.

And then she realized what she'd said. "Ex-wife. I'm Merk's ex-wife," she said hurriedly. "My name is Katina Marshal."

"Welcome, Katina. We made a place for you at the table, so come and sit down." In a smooth voice Ice turned to Merk and said, a twinkle shining in her eyes, "Merk, get your wife a coffee."

Katina winced. "Sorry, Merk."

With an irritable shrug, he said, "They were bound to find out sometime. So, whatever."

But would they? If they were surprised, it meant he hadn't told them about what happened eleven years ago. When Katina finally sat, Merk handed her a large cup of coffee. Black just the way she liked. She wondered at that. She had remembered all kinds of little things about him too. Deciding not to bring it up, she huddled over the cup and blew on the top. She'd really like to drink it, but it was hot.

When they were all seated, that air of expectation hung over the table. She looked at Merk and shrugged.

He just said, "You brought it up. You explain."

Her eyebrows shot up toward her hairline. "I would rather we not have to. Isn't it obvious? We were married. Now we're divorced. It's a closed book."

"How long ago was this?" Ice asked curiously. "I've known Merk for a long time."

Katina laughed. "When we were both dumb and stupid. As in Vegas stupid, eleven years ago."

That startled a laugh out of everyone at the table. Merk just rolled his eyes. She grinned. "Hey, the Elvis Presley Wedding Chapel was damn good that night."

"Yeah, how many margaritas did it take for that to look good?" Merk teased her.

Under the glare of fascination from everybody around them, she shrugged and confessed, "I don't remember." That brought everybody into full gales of laughter.

Sheepishly she grinned and said, "Still, when I ran into trouble, I knew exactly who to call." She looked across at Merk and said, "Thank you for saving my life today."

As a conversation stopper, it was a killer. Complete silence swept through the room.

"YOU'RE WELCOME." MERK studied Katina across the table. It was a weird bridge across time. That same simple honestly had caught and held on to him the first time he'd met her. He even remembered what it was—something to do with standing before a card table in Vegas and her turning to him and saying she didn't even know how to play. He'd taught her right then and there. Of course, before the end of the night, they'd been teaching each other plenty. "You ready to tell us what this is all about?"

She stared down at her coffee cup, afraid to lift her gaze

to the others. "I don't know any of you. If you're all part of this private security company, maybe you can handle yourselves…better than I can obviously. But this is very dangerous. I don't want to put anybody else in the cross-hairs."

Ice reached an arm across to Katina's shoulder and gave her a gentle hug. "I wouldn't worry about that. We've taken on some of the most dangerous jobs in the world."

Merk watched as Katina studied Ice's face, then she looked at him for confirmation. He nodded his head. "We're all ex-military," he said. "Levi formed this company with Ice, and we're still doing what we did before, only privately now."

Katina slowly relaxed, like the starch had gone out of her shirt. "I really was right to call you, wasn't I?"

He nodded. "Although I'm curious as to why you did. We haven't spoken in over ten years."

"You were headed for special military training after Vegas. Did you go?"

He nodded. "I did indeed."

"And I was hoping that, if you had, maybe you'd know what I was supposed to do"

"That's where I met a lot of these people. But now it's time for you to come clean. Just what the hell have you gotten yourself into?"

She glanced around the table and said, "Some of it's a little bit personal, so just bear with me." She glanced over at Merk, then dropped her gaze quickly.

He leaned forward and laid his hand out on the table. She stretched across and placed hers on it. Just as she had eleven years ago. He marveled at how small and yet capable that hand was.

She took a deep breath and said, "When I got back from Vegas, the ink wasn't dry on my wedding certificate, was even less so on our divorce papers, which we had to wait one year to file," she said, interjecting a note of humor.

"I took stock of my life. I'd gone to Vegas to celebrate my twenty-first birthday and didn't really like what I did while I was under the influence. I hadn't been much of a drinker but of course, turning twenty-one was a big deal. When I went home, I completed college and got an associate's degree in bookkeeping. I decided I wanted to do more, so I got my accounting degree. I worked for several small companies initially. And then finally, about four years ago, I was hired to work for Bristol and Partners, Ltd., a real estate property management company with an office in Houston."

She glanced around the table, wondering if anyone knew the name. Some people nodded and she continued.

"At first everything seemed to be simple and normal. Of course, I was in a junior accounting position, and we had several senior accountants in the company as it was a large business, with many locations nationwide. In this last year I was moving up the ranks. About four months ago, one of the accountants took an extended leave and I was asked to step in temporarily until she got back on her feet."

She stopped talking. Merk gently stroked her fingers and said in a low voice, "It's okay. Tell us the rest."

She shrugged. "Well, once I did, everything went downhill."

Chapter 5

S HE REALLY SHOULDN'T tell them more. She looked around at all the hard-looking men and even stone-cold Ice—aptly named—beside her. She had no idea who they all were, although quick introductions had been made. Making the wrong decision here could get someone killed. Merk squeezed her fingers in that indomitable way and said, "Continue."

"Well, I imagine you can guess the rest," she said. "I found a few discrepancies, shall I say." She waved her free hand in the air dismissively and said, "Not anything major but just a little bit more than I was comfortable with, and I didn't quite know how to handle it. I sat on the information for a while and then decided to see if the original accountant had just made a simple bookkeeping error, because that certainly can happen, particularly when we're talking about large sums of money. When I backtracked, I found a few other things wrong."

"Big-dollar figures?" Ice asked.

"Yes. Tens of millions of dollars."

They all nodded as if they had expected that.

Katina continued. "If I'd followed the company line, maybe nothing would have happened with this. I was supposed to go to my boss and tell him what I'd found. Let him deal with it." She broke off again.

"But you didn't?" Merk asked.

She shook her head. "No, and what I did was probably worse. I have copies of everything I saw."

They all straightened up.

She winced. "I was afraid I would get blamed for this misallocation. It would have been so easy to frame me for some of this, after doing the woman's job for months." She shook her head, knowing some of this was definitely jail-type stuff. White-collar crime it might be, but a lot of money was being moved. "I didn't want to take the fall for it."

"That's certainly understandable," Merk said. "But in all seriousness, if you have that information, it's very important that you hand it over to the authorities."

"I know that." She stared down at her coffee and wondered if they believed her, if she should tell them the rest. But if she didn't, how else did she explain why she hadn't already told the police when she'd been at the station today?

"Tell us the rest," Merk said firmly. "We can't help if we don't know all of it. You can't keep something like this to yourself. It'll eat you inside out."

She lifted her head and let her gaze slip around the group. Her stare stopped at a new arrival in the doorway. This woman didn't have the same look as Ice at all. A second joined her. She looked about as hard as a cotton ball.

Katina frowned and tilted her head toward the doorway. Merk turned and said, "Sienna, Lissa, come join us."

Lissa said, "We don't want to disturb you. It sounds like it might be personal."

Stone, the largest man in the room—and that said a lot—stood up and reached out a hand. She walked over, grabbed it, and he tugged her into a spot at the table beside him. "This is a mix of business and personal." He grinned.

"Merk's ex-wife has come to him for help."

Lissa spun round and gasped. "You're laughing about that? She's in trouble. You have to help her. You did me."

As if he got the rise out of her he wanted, Stone turned toward the group as he draped his huge arm around her shoulders. "That's what we're discussing, whether we can do anything. To decide wisely, we need the rest of the story. So sit quietly. Let's listen." His focus zinged over to Katina. "The floor is yours again."

Katina dropped her gaze to the table, barely hiding her worry. Really she could do nothing else but ask for help. She had to tell somebody. Shit, she didn't know why she trusted these people, but they looked capable of handling anything.

She looked up to find Merk studying her carefully. "I found a notebook in the accountant's drawers. Like a code book. I didn't understand it all, well any of it actually as it wasn't standard accounting procedures," she said. "I found a list of names—or short forms of them—and beside a couple were written the word *cop*. So I'm assuming some policemen are involved in this mess, but I don't know who or which ones, or how high ranking they are. Presumably those on the lower end don't have the kind of money for what's going on here."

She reached up and pinched the bridge of her nose. "But that's my personal judgment. A lot of people have money we don't know about. Just because they don't work in a high-paying job, doesn't mean they don't have extensive portfolios."

"Do you remember the names?"

"They weren't complete, just short forms. Like … *TMET14—cop*." She glanced around to see if that made sense to anybody, but blank faces stared back at her. "Like I said, I don't know what it means, or if her usage of the word *cop* means something else entirely, like an acronym of some sort."

"Good reason to be worried about the authorities involved," Levi said.

She asked, "Am I just paranoid?" Her gaze circled the room, hoping someone had an answer.

Ice snorted. "You were snatched in a parking lot. They tied you up, threw you in the back of a van, with the kidnappers proceeding in a high-speed car chase to evade Merk and the cops. And you're making light of it or dismissing it as just your imagination?"

Laid out that way, it made her sound foolish. "Not until after I got the phone calls and emails did I get really worried."

"Whoa. What emails? What phone calls?" Merk asked. "Let's go back to where you found this information. Exactly what did you do and what happened from that time? And how long ago was this?"

"A couple months ago, I found the first entry that didn't make any sense. I knew I was really onto something seriously crooked last month though." She stared at Merk, gaining strength from the support in his gaze. "I didn't do anything for the longest time because I'd never been in this situation before and didn't know what to do. But then I heard rumors that the accountant was returning since she had recovered from some car accident. That's when I knew I had to act because I wouldn't have access to any of this information again.

"So one day I'd been complaining at work about having a hectic week—on purpose, to give myself a cover story to stay late in the office," she said with a sigh. "Instead I copied and saved as much of the information as I could to a USB key without raising any alarms."

"And you didn't tell anyone?" Levi asked.

She shook her head. "No, again I didn't know who to tell. I was afraid to go to the wrong person. Or, if I went in and made a full disclosure, this huge internal investigation would go nowhere, but I'd be blamed. Or maybe my company would fold, and they'd come after me." She leaned forward slightly, looking at their faces. "At no time did I think I was in serious danger because honestly, I didn't think anybody knew what I had found."

Merk said, "But somebody obviously did."

She shrugged. "I guess, but I don't know how they would've." She clasped her hands together and continued the story. "The accountant came back, and I returned to my normal position. But I had all this information, and I retained her login so if I needed to, I could go back in. But I was pretty sure the accountant would change it her first day back." Then Katina stopped. Expectation hung in the air around her. "I wanted to see if she had deleted the information, because if so, I wasn't sure anything I had would stand up in its place. In fact, I didn't want to login again at all because I had no business in that corner of the world in terms of the company files."

She fell silent.

"But you did anyway," Merk said drily. "Didn't you realize that would likely trigger somebody's interest? It's one thing when you were filling in at her desk—although that kind of extracurricular activity shouldn't have been allowed either—but if you had gone in after the accountant was back, and she had changed her login, they would know somebody else was accessing the information."

"I *know* that. I didn't do it again," she reassured him. "The only reason I had access to those files was because she kept it on the company network, not her private computer. I have access to the network to do my own job and so when working in her files, I found the login to her protected ones. Once I realized what was going on, then I went looking for more and...found it."

Everyone sat back and stared at her. She shrugged. "However, afterward it seemed as if I was suddenly under somebody's watchful eye. I'd get called to the head office a little more often. When I got up and went for coffee breaks, I felt like people were watching me. When I went to the lunchroom, almost always somebody would be there, suddenly sitting with me—where in the past I would be alone. Nobody before had ever given a shit about who I was, where I was, or what I was doing." She winced. "For a long time I thought I was imagining things."

"Is there any chance, because of your new position, that others wanted to get closer to you?" Lissa asked curiously. "The higher up the food chain you move, the more others want to rub off some of that shaker-mover energy from you."

"Oh, now that's an interesting idea," Sienna said.

Katina looked at the two women and realized just how different their mind-sets were from the men. These two weren't military, but were more in tune with the popular or common man.

"I never considered that," Katina admitted. "I suppose it's a possibility. People were certainly friendlier after I took over the top accountant position. But as it's not something that I would do, it never occurred to me somebody else would."

"Did anybody at work ever threaten you or make you

feel that way?" Merk asked.

She shook her head. "No. I figured I got away with it." The corner of her lips quirked downward. "Of course I should've known better. People who dabble in corruption and fraud obviously have some safeguards in place. But the longer everything went along smoothly, the more comfortable I felt."

"Until ..." Merk prodded her.

"Until I got a strange email one day, and the subject line just asked *Where is it?* The body of the email was blank, sent from some generic social-networking site. I didn't know who it came from. No name was attached, just a series of numbers." She spread her hands, palms up. "I have no idea what the email meant. I didn't take anything. No"—she switched her wording—"I copied information, but I didn't remove any."

"So maybe they wanted the USB key you downloaded the data to."

Katina studied the man who'd spoken for the first time. He wasn't as big as the others, with dark hair and brows, but pure-white skin. He looked to be just as knowing and knowledgeable as the rest of them. She thought his name was Harrison.

"Maybe. But how would they know I put the info on one?"

"Hidden cameras for one but a keystroke capture— keylogging—would be my guess for all of it," Ice said. She shrugged. "Honestly, if they have a decent IT department, they should be able to find out what you did, when, and on what computer within minutes. If they can't, they aren't worth their paychecks.

Katina was sure her expression told everyone in this

room how little she knew about what Ice just said. Thankfully, Ice continued so the focus was off Katina's bewildered look.

"I understand professional accounting has checks and balances inherent in its system to catch basic human errors."

"That's very true," Katina said.

"However," Ice went on, "if you add in a tech-savvy CEO, maybe a boss who has dealt with embezzling employees before, then a third safeguarding layer could be in play."

Katina shook her head. "Not my boss. Not Robert. He's more of a salesman. He loves to interact with his employees, with people in general."

Ice raised one finger, her mouth a grim line. "Maybe so, but if the bad guys are one of those lower-level accountants, trying to sneak stuff by Robert, then things can get really intricate."

When everyone just stared at Ice, she shook her head and added, "I listen when Bullard speaks." She turned toward Katina to explain. "Bullard's expertise is in security hardware and software."

Katina nodded her thanks.

"Plus," Levi added, "it's common knowledge that you can't email information without leaving a trail. Even through the network to another location would've been traceable. And the easiest and most available method for data transfer would be a USB drive under normal circumstances."

She studied Levi's face and winced.

"I suppose that's possible. But why didn't they say something when it first happened or even when I gave notice?"

"Maybe it only came to light once that head accountant had returned, and it could've been a week or two after you left that she realized even the remote possibility that you had found this because she'd left that information accessible. Maybe she thought she'd get into trouble. Consider what it's like when you return to a job or begin a new one, which in this case, would mean she'd have a ton of catching up to do. And she might not have considered that you would find her private files."

Harrison spoke up again. "But it would've been easy enough for her to have seen the last time they were accessed, and she'd have realized what happened while you were there. For a while everyone might've even considered you didn't know what you had actually seen."

"In their mind, you're a junior accountant and possibly couldn't understand the material in front of you," Levi said. "But by then, it becomes a worry. Something they couldn't quite let go. And they followed you to see what you did with the information."

"From the time the accountant came back, how long before you felt like you were being watched?" Merk asked.

She flicked her gaze in his direction. "I can't be sure exactly, but maybe one or two weeks." She pursed her lips and thought about it a little harder. "The thing is, like Levi said, I was also really swamped because I had returned to my position which was no longer in the same shape I had left it and had a lot of work to fix, so I'm not sure I noticed right away. Maybe they were on to me fairly quickly."

"It doesn't really matter though," Levi said. "The fact is, we have to assume they know you have a copy of this information."

"And you said there were phone calls and more emails."

She nodded quickly. "Almost the same email came in repeatedly afterward. The numbers on the top were different as to whom it was from, but it was always addressed to me at work and had the same subject line, nothing else. And then they came to my personal email." She glanced over at Merk again. "That's when I really freaked out."

"Sure, but it wouldn't have been hard to find that, particularly if they've already accessed your business email and quite likely that computer because most people check their personal email at work anyway."

She considered that and winced once more. "Yeah, I did. Not often, but every once in a while. I'm very touchy about my stuff though. I've never been that trusting."

"The minute you opened that program and logged in, they had your email, and contacts," the dark-haired man said. "After that it was pretty simple to get anything else they wanted."

"But how did they know I was meeting Merk at the pub? Oh my God, my phone." She immediately stood and searched her pockets for it. "Merk, did you see my phone?"

"I took it before coming here in case they were tracking us with it. You were sleeping so I didn't wake you to ask. No signal can escape that box." He nodded toward a metal box at the end of the table.

She frowned and stared at it. "How did you know to do that?"

"Easy. Planting GPS trackers is what any of us would've done had our situations been reversed. Some phones come with their own built-in, but we would add one to be sure in most cases. We bug the phone so we can hear conversations and generally track the person."

"I'll give you a burner phone with a new number. No one can track you then." He smiled at her. "It's okay. This is what we do."

She stared at him in shock.

"You're safe here." Ice reached over and patted her hand. "Even if you were tracked to this compound, we have a disturbance setting that sends out a jamming signal. It stops anything within from being tracked."

There was a beat of silence.

Katina gazed back at the box, realizing the small red light on its side was now off.

Merk got up, walked around, opened it, and took out the phone. "Rhodes, got your tools with you to open this?"

The man called Rhodes stood up and walked around, pulling out a small tool kit from his pocket. The two men bent over the phone and proceeded to open it.

She'd never seen the inside of her phone, and couldn't really get a glimpse of it from where she was, but Merk reached over with a pair of tweezers and plucked out a small piece of metal. He held it up for the others to see. "Got it."

"Is that a tracker?"

"Well, it was. Now it's just a dead piece of technology."

He dropped it into the metal box and put her phone back together. He turned it on and held it in front of her so she could see it was working. She couldn't understand how someone had managed to get it in her phone. She'd wondered if she had been tracked to the parking lot by the men who kidnapped her, but still considered it impossible for somebody to have gotten to her phone and done this.

"It would have been an easy matter to wait for a moment when you had your back turned, even a short trip to the ladies' room, for them to have installed that," Ice said quietly in answer to her unspoken question.

"I guess you just never really know who you are dealing with and what's happening around you, do you?" Katina asked. "So does that mean my car has bugs as well?"

Rhodes laughed. "We have some detectors that will let us know if any are close by. If it was me, I'd have put one in there." He smacked Merk on the shoulder and walked out.

She turned her gaze to Merk and said, "Is he going to check?"

Merk nodded. "He'll have an answer for you soon enough."

"But I didn't want to bring the danger here to you," she wailed. "I didn't want anyone else getting involved. Do you see how dangerous this is? Why don't you just let me get my car and go?"

He turned and stared at her. Instead of the warm, friendly smile she'd seen earlier, the stark, flat gaze bore deep into her own as if seeing through the darkness of the last weeks, into the heart of her. "You really think I would let you take off after what happened to you? I knew there was a damn good possibility you were being tracked. I went through a lot today to save your ass," he snapped. "Like hell I'll let something happen to you now."

"That means they can follow us here. And that means people know where I am."

"Good. Let them come." As if too pissed to trust himself, he turned and stormed from the room.

She glared after him, understanding the feeling. She had no place to go. An uncomfortable silence took over the room. As they studied her, she turned to face them and said quietly, "I'm very sorry for any trouble I brought to your doorstep. It was never my intention." She turned her glare back to the doorway again and added, "I did tell Merk I wanted to be alone so I could just run, but he wouldn't listen."

"Good," Ice said. "That's not how we operate."

But Katina didn't know how they did things here.

MERK HEADED TO Katina's car where he watched Rhodes go over it. "See anything?"

"I've found one, but the meter's saying two."

"I'll check under the hood," Merk said.

But before he got there, Rhodes said, "Removed that one." He bent down and snagged the small item from underneath the running board behind the back wheel. He held it up, then turned the small meter in his hand toward the front of the car.

Together they poured over the engine, following the signal from hot to cold and found it just underneath the radiator. "This one was hidden better. It could easily have been missed."

They ran the meter around the vehicle again to confirm nothing else was here and then shut it down. Taking the trackers back to the shop, they added them to the box.

Merk turned to look back at her car. The hood and trunk were still open. He walked over and realized her bags were inside. A lot of them, as if she'd packed for a long trip. In fact, he was pretty damn sure she'd been planning to run. So why the hell did she call him in the first place? Maybe that was the best question he needed to ask her. The rest could wait. But if she was already running, why even bother letting him know?

He stormed back into the kitchen and stood in the doorway. Everyone was talking, but more about general topics, like the weather and type of cookies they had in their hands. He frowned when he saw them. Trust Alfred to bring out treats for company. Merk had been craving cookies for days, and Alfred had just smiled in that benign way of his.

Merk snagged one and said, "First question, and it's maybe the most important of all. If you were ready to run, and I can see from all the bags in the back of your car that you weren't planning on returning, why even bother calling me?"

She stared at him, and then he felt like a heel as her bottom lip trembled.

"I was afraid." She stopped to catch her breath. He could hear the tremor in her voice. "I was afraid they'd kill me, and nobody would know."

"Shit." What a hell of a statement, and it said a lot about the lonely state of her life if she called him just for that.

"I don't have many friends, just one or two, and not much family. My parents divorced, remarried, and redivorced." She made a face. "I don't have any relationship with them. And, as tenuous a connection as it might be, you are my ex-husband. I didn't know who else to call and was ... still am, afraid to bring trouble to anyone's doorstep."

"So we would have had lunch, and you'd tell me bad guys were after you and then say, *If they kill me, hey, you'll know why I'm dead?*" he asked incredulously. "Does that make any sense?"

She shrugged. "I don't admit to having any common sense lately," she cried. "I've been reacting, not thinking, trying to stay alive and ahead of these guys. I needed help. I didn't know who to go to. I realized I had no reason to believe you really could help, but I just thought, maybe if I touched base one more time, then at least you'd know, if you never saw me again, then chances were I was gone."

"And how would I know if I never saw you again, when I haven't seen you in eleven years?" he snapped. He ran his hands through his hair, wondering why she'd do that, and then he stopped. He walked closer, his gaze on her. "You have it on you, don't you? You intended to give it to me."

He stood towering over her, hating when she cowered from him. He knew he was right. Now, instead of wanting to know why she'd called him, he desperately needed to know why she hadn't given him whatever it was she had.

Merk shoved his face closer to hers and said, his voice as soft as he could make it, "So why didn't you?"

Her lips trembled, and her eyes were bright with tears, but she stayed strong. "Because whoever has it is in danger, and I won't do that to you."

He threw up his hands in frustration and glared at her. "You are just as frustrating today as you were years ago."

"And you're just as domineering and arrogant and force-ful today as you were then," she shouted at him.

He stared at her and grinned. "We were good together, weren't we?"

"Oh, yeah, so good, that it lasted one night." She reached up with both hands, grabbing her hair, and snapped, "I don't know what I was thinking. I should never have contacted you. We don't even like each other."

"Oh, I like you just fine." Merk smiled. "I especially like the new model, but that's got nothing to do with it. You came to me because you knew I would help. And now, for whatever dumb reason, you're afraid I'll get hurt if I do."

"And that's because I like you too," she admitted. "And I like the new model better as well." She stood so she could face him squarely, but as short as she was, she couldn't gain any height on him. So she stepped atop the bench with her good leg, easing the other slowly there, and stared at him. Planting her hands on her hips, she said, "I can't let anybody

I like die because of my stupidity."

Ignoring the very real presence of the others in the room, he reached over, snagged her into his arms, and kissed her.

Hard.

She pulled herself free and cried, "Oh, no, you don't. That's what got us into trouble in the first place!"

He laughed. "That's what took us to bed," he corrected. "But what got us into marital trouble, well, I'll blame the booze for that."

"You could be right there. I haven't had tequila since," she confessed. She grinned at him. "It was quite a shock waking up the next day married."

"Ditto," he admitted. "But we fixed it and put it behind us. Until I got the bloody phone call from you."

She winced. "Here I go apologizing again. I should never have called you."

He hooked his finger under her chin and lifted it so she faced him. "If you say that one more time …"

Immediately she fisted her hands on her hips once more and glared into his face. "And what will you do about it?"

With their noses inches apart, he said in a very low whisper, "I'll do the same damn thing I did back then."

She gasped and immediately backed up. "No, you won't." She shook her head fast. "No more shenanigans out of you." She turned her back on him, stepped off the bench, and sat back down again.

He chuckled and realized how much of a spectacle the others had just enjoyed. "Don't get used to this," he said to his team. "We're not entertaining you people forever."

Sienna chuckled. "That's okay. Seems an awful lot of stuff is between you two that you should deal with. Then you can move forward in your relationship, like you're supposed to."

Instantly Katina shook her head yet again. "No relationship. We don't have one," she said a little too emphatically. "We aren't going to."

Merk stared down at her and wondered. All the same things that attracted him to her a long time ago were still there. She was feisty, fiery, and cute. And of course, now that she was in trouble, it appealed to his protective instincts all that much more. Maybe, just maybe, they should reconsider whether they wanted to rekindle their relationship.

Not like there were any barriers to it. They had their whole lives ahead of them. He tucked that little tidbit in the back of his brain and then smiled at Sienna.

"Time you took a little closer look to home in terms of relationships," he suggested.

She glanced at him blankly and in confusion asked, "What are you talking about? I don't have a relationship right now."

His grin widened and he said, "Yet."

Just then Rhodes walked inside and said, "You coming out to grab these bags for her, Merk, or not?" He stood in the doorway in exasperation. "I waited for you to come back, not sit here and play with your lady friend."

Merk watched Sienna as her gaze darted to Rhodes in the doorway wnd Merk saw the subtle shift. The interest, the softening of her features, tilted lips, and then a smile. When her gaze drifted past his, Merk deepened his grin, and with a tiny almost imperceptible nod toward Rhodes, he said, "Exactly."

For a moment she didn't understand what he meant, and then she got it.

Fiery red flushed over her pale skin. "Oh, no you don't.

No way are you pinning that on me." She rose, picked up her cup of coffee, and said, "Enough of that crap or I'll dock your paycheck." She turned and walked from the room.

Rhodes stepped up and said, "Boy, what did you do to upset her?"

"Nothing. Just pointed out her future."

Everybody else in the room chuckled.

Rhodes stared at him, then everyone else, and asked suspiciously, "What is this, an inside joke?"

"Maybe. No need to worry though, with time you'll become part of the joke too." He hooked an arm around his buddy's shoulders and said, "Come on. Let's go grab those bags. And we'll tuck Katina into one of the spare rooms."

Behind him he could hear Katina cry out, "I'm not staying …"

"Yes, you are." And he headed to her car where they retrieved five bags.

When they had everything, they checked the front, including the glove box, and then walked back into the kitchen.

"Ice, any idea where we should put her?"

"Nowhere," Katina snapped.

But Ice stood in that smooth elegant motion that was so her and said, "A room has been prepped for her already." She smiled at Katina. "Come this way."

Chapter 6

"WHAT THE HELL am I doing here?" Katina murmured to herself as she wandered around the small bedroom.

She wasn't a prisoner. She hadn't been locked in. So why then did she feel like she had no choice but to stay here? She doubted Merk would enforce a prisonlike existence, but they'd all made this decision whether she liked it or not. And she didn't like it.

She also knew Merk was pissed at her. With good reason. She plunked down on the bed and flopped backward, her arms over her head.

Should she give it to them? She reached up and scrubbed her face, willing her exhausted brain to work. But her leg ached again, and her thoughts were definitely fogging up. She hadn't gotten much sleep in the last several weeks. The last few nights had been really bad.

After all, she'd been planning her escape.

And now everything had come to a dead stop. As if she'd jumped, but, instead of leaping off a cliff, she'd only managed to jump halfway *to* the cliff. And now somehow the cliff had been removed. She was left suspended in midair.

She remembered in Vegas how she hadn't had a doubt with Merk around. He'd been a powerhouse, even back then, and she'd fallen willingly into any plan he'd come up with.

They'd gone from game table to bar to the pub to the streets, laughing and cheering and crying, and had had the time of their lives. Whatever he suggested she'd gone for. She hadn't been coerced, but it had been so different. He'd been a magnet, and she felt that pull even now. She'd been delighted to be with him. That kind of power, that kind of self-confidence was sexy.

She'd fallen into instant lust with the man. They'd had one hell of a night. But by the cold dawn of the next day ... make that noon when they'd both woken up to realize what they'd done, well, she'd backed off and had been scared to find herself with anybody quite so powerful and dominant. Apparently she didn't have any brains when it came to him. She just fell completely susceptible to his whims.

Look at what happened today. Merk had no problem getting her to do what he wanted. And she wasn't going through that again. She'd learned her lesson—she hoped she had. But after today, maybe not.

There was a knock on the door. "Katina, it's Merk. Let me in."

She gave a half snort as she lay there. That was so him. No request, not even a question, more that he was entitled to come in. But not a direct order, just that you-will-do-what-I-say type of command. The trouble was her. She was already on her feet and walking to the door, which she flung open. "What is it about you that I just do everything you tell me to do?" she snapped.

His eyebrows shot up in surprise at the greeting, but he answered amiably. "At least you understand when it's imperative that you do something. That's important, instead of protesting and causing trouble for the sake of being difficult."

He gave her a gentle nudge, and she stepped back into her room. Instantly he followed and closed the door behind them. He glanced around the small space and smiled.

"They've done a hell of a nice job in this place. We have guest rooms that aren't just small holes in the walls and bunk beds tacked onto the plywood."

She walked over to the only chair and sat down. She had no idea what he was talking about with plywood and guest rooms, but she assumed he was just making conversation. Only she was tired. "Why are you here?"

He sat down on the side of the bed and studied her. "Where did you hide it?"

Immediately she crossed her arms over her chest and slouched deeper into the soft chair. "It's not safe for you to have it."

Instead of arguing with her, he gave her a smile that was gentle in understanding. "I guess you still like me then," he teased.

She glared at him. "Don't you dare do that lethal stuff again! I fell for your charms once. I'm not going there again."

He chuckled. She found herself smiling anyway.

"The thing is, as long as you're hiding it, we can't do anything about the men after you," he said. "If you give it to us, we can make copies to send to the right people."

She chewed on her bottom lip and worried on the problem. He was right. If something happened to her, those people would get away with it—and her murder—and no one would be held accountable. As much as she hated that, she didn't want them to go after Merk or the others and to hurt more victims due to her foolishness.

Only Merk wasn't giving her much of a chance to think about it. He leaned across the space, picked up her hand, and held it between his. The heat of his palm burned into her slightly cold skin. Shit, she didn't realize just how tired she was, or how stressed, until she felt the absolute comfort of the warmth of his hand and just knowing that somebody was here to help out.

"I didn't say thank-you for saving me. I didn't expect you to show up," she said. "When I was in the parking lot for so long, I figured you'd stood me up," she confessed. "And then all I could think about was that maybe that was you in the parking lot, after they threw me in the back of the van, and maybe you'd seen what happened, and maybe, just maybe, you would know what to do to help me."

She shook her head. "It never occurred to me you'd be quite so capable as to not only contact those who needed to be contacted but to also keep up the wild car chase and track me down to eventually rescue me." She smiled at him. "I guess all that military training did you some good."

"You did thank me for saving your life," he reminded her. "But you can't distract me from the main conversation."

She glared at him. "I don't know what I want to do."

He nodded. "Understandable. You're scared. You don't know who to trust, and you don't want to make the wrong decision."

"Exactly. If I make the wrong decision, the consequences are huge."

"And if you make the right decision, the consequences are also huge."

They stared at each other across the short distance, her hands, both of them now, cradled gently in his much bigger ones. She stared down at them and said, "As long as you promise to hand it all over to the right authorities and let them deal with it."

"I promise. You do realize that won't necessarily save you though, right?"

She nodded. "Unless they know you have already handed it all over … Then the game is up. The men will just get the hell out of the country themselves."

He laughed. "In our experience, the bad guys generally think it all works out in their favor, so they continue on. And they end up doing things in a very stupid way."

She sighed heavily. "I was hoping they'd be the kind to just run."

"And they might depend on the ties they have in another countries, if it's money laundering and tax fraud. Who knows? But they crossed the line when they kidnapped you, so what else is going on? Because, if anything more serious is involved, they won't hesitate to come after you again."

"Then we have to leave," she cried. "And now."

"We're leaving in the morning. You need to rest and to heal, to calm down and to breathe."

She looked up at him and hated that her eyes stung with tears yet unshed. "It just seems like I've been running for so long," she whispered. "Once that first email came through, I was living in a never-ending nightmare." She gave a broken laugh. "No, actually it was when I found those accounting discrepancies. … I felt trapped, like I just had no good options."

He tugged her forward into his arms and held her close against his chest—finally making her aware of the shivers wracking her body. His big arms were wrapped securely around her, as if he could instill the warmth and calm of his own physical body on hers.

Like that would happen. The only thing that ever evolved when they got this close together was the burning up of the sheets. Although considering she was cold, maybe that wasn't such a bad idea. She almost smiled, then remembered the circumstances that had brought them together again. She pulled back. "I'll talk to you in the morning. I should be able to pick it up then without any trouble."

He nodded.

She could hear the unasked questions in the air, but she refused to give into them. She wouldn't tell him where it was right now.

"We must determine where to copy and disperse the duplicates." She leaned back so she could look at his face. "Before we head out and collect it, we need a list of who it's going to. Plus a laptop and a post office printer because I don't want just electronic copies. We need physical copies." She frowned, thinking as hard as her sore brain would allow. "And a secure place to do that, with no one looking over our shoulders."

She fell silent. Not understanding fully her hesitation to tell him where it was. Maybe … because she was so damn tired and couldn't think straight. But it was like that damn key was poison. As soon as she touched that, shit went wrong.

HE DIDN'T KNOW how to get her to trust him. They really needed to get their hands on that information. Not that he gave a damn about it, but he knew, as long as she was the only one who held it, she was in danger. The sooner they spread the truth to those who could help, the sooner she'd be safer. Although he was pretty damn sure that the prosecution would want her as a witness in the event of a trial, and, once anything like kidnapping became involved, it would be a big deal all around. But he also didn't want those copies in the wrong hands. Therefore, they had to be careful who they picked.

"It's almost time for dinner," he said, checking his watch. "Let's go downstairs and discuss the list over our meal, figure out who we should send all the information to."

"It's not that I don't trust everybody here, but it seems like we're taking a big risk involving so many."

He smiled down at her and dropped a kiss on her forehead. "If it was any other group, I'd say you were perfectly right to be concerned. But, as it's this group, my team, my unit from the military, and the few women that we have involved," he said, "your information is perfectly safe here. Not one of them would betray us."

She smiled. "Okay. So is it safe to say I'm starving then?"

He laughed. Once she set her feet gently on the ground, he stood up and held out a hand. "Trust me enough to do this," he said with a smile. "I was honorable the last time we saw each other."

She gave a delicate half snort. "Yeah, at least you married me then."

At that, he burst into laughter. He led her down the hallway. "You know, I have wondered over the years where you were, what you'd done, and if we would ever meet again," he said. "But I never thought I would look back and remember how much fun we had during that time in our lives."

She turned and tossed him a teasing grin. "Now that it's eleven years behind us, it's easy to laugh. Back then ... not so much."

"Did you ever tell anybody?"

"No." She gasped in horror. "Well, I told Anna, my best

friend, a little bit but not all of it. You know what they all would've said if they'd known." She shook her head. "Silence was the only option." But her voice carried a teasing note as she said it.

"There's nothing to be ashamed of, you know."

She laughed. "Also nothing to be proud of. Figuring out how many drinks it took to get to the bottom of a bottle is really not the goal I wanted to set in my life."

The others were already in the dining room. This time, instead of them just sitting around hugging cups of coffee, Alfred had filled the center of the table with roast chicken and vegetables. And a great big Caesar salad alongside it all.

Merk grinned. "My kind of meal."

"If it's food, it's edible, and it won't walk away on me, it's my kind of meal," Katina said.

He stopped in his tracks and looked at her. "That's why you went to Vegas. ... You could eat cheap down there."

She shook her finger at him. "You forgot, drink cheap too."

With everyone at the table, and the lighthearted atmosphere, they all dug into solid food. It was one magic Alfred knew very well. Whenever they were active on a job or needed to be ready to go in an instant, he got their bodies filled with really good healthy food.

As soon as they all dished up their selections and settled down to eat, Merk said, "Katina has agreed to take me to the data. However, first she wants to see a list of who gets the information. Before we leave the house, she wants to know where we will copy this material, print it out, then send both email and snail-mail copies of it all at the same time."

Ice looked at Katina and nodded her head. "Good decision," she said. "But you're safest place is here."

"That's what Merk said too," Katina said. "But we already know my vehicle has been tracked to this place. Therefore, they could come looking for me here. And I don't want them to find it."

Levi and Ice exchanged glances. Merk watched them, wondering what they were up to.

Then Levi turned to look at them directly. "Merk, what about Gunner, Logan's dad? He lives in Houston. He's ex-military, upper brass. His place is like a small Fort Knox. Logan went into the military because of his father. I'd ask Logan to take you, but he's in California doing the guard-duty detail."

Merk snorted at that. "Right. Maybe ask him if that would be possible."

Levi shook his head. "I'll call direct."

"You sure it's safe to bring another person into this?" Katina asked quietly. "I don't want anyone else to get involved."

"True," Levi said cheerfully. "But, if Gunner thought we were protecting him, he wouldn't be happy. And he was always a man looking to help a damsel in distress ..."

"Isn't that the truth?" Merk said with a smile. "He misses the military, in a big way. He was secret ops. But now retired he's bored as hell."

Merk looked at Levi and said, "Good call." He pulled out a notepad and pen, putting it on the table beside him, then said to the room in general, "Names. Who are we sending this information to? Talking fraud, offshore accounts, possible money-laundering. Kidnapping. But who is it that we trust to look into this safely?"

"The new DA in Houston is good." Ice reached across the table for the jug of water and filled her glass. "Formerly from California. I remember hearing good words about him. He closed a lot of high-profile corruption cases."

"I don't know him at all, but I'll take your word for it." Merk wrote down his name on the list. Then he wrote down Gunner. "Gunner probably has other people to suggest we contact as well."

"If there was a military angle to this, then I'd suggest Commander Jackson. Or just Jackson, as he is known now," Rhodes said quietly from the far side of the table.

Stone added his agreement. "He's always been straight with us."

"He might be worth contacting anyway. Remember he's still in the military, just not the same department, so he has a long reach."

The conversation carried on for another forty-five minutes until Merk had six names.

Then Ice said, "What about Bullard?"

Merk stopped and stared at her. "You think Bullard would know somebody, or are you saying we should include him in this?"

"That man surprises everyone. He knows a lot of people. In a case like this, he might very well have a good idea of who we can trust." Ice took a sip of her water and said, "I'll call him after dinner."

At that point, Alfred cleared off the plates with everyone's help, and then came back with a cheesecake. It was Katina's comment that made everyone grin.

"Oh, my God, I've died and gone to heaven."

"No, my dear, the whole point of this is to not have you die and go to heaven," Alfred said with a cheeky grin before he turned to grab a bunch of smaller plates and dessert forks off the sideboard.

Chapter 7

Aᴀꜰᴛᴇʀ ᴅɪɴɴᴇʀ, Kᴀᴛɪɴᴀ didn't know what to do with herself. She offered to help clean up the kitchen and wash dishes, but Alfred scooted her out of his area. She'd wandered into the huge living room with several different sitting areas but found it empty. Merk caught up with her a few minutes later, after she'd sat down in front of a large gas fireplace that wasn't turned on.

"There you are," Merk said, startling her with his sudden arrival. "I wasn't exactly sure where you went to. Levi's contacting Gunner. Ice will call Bullard, and Stone and Lissa are moving into one of our newly completed apartments. They've been unpacking just these last few days, so they're in turmoil." He shrugged. "Everyone has normal lives to live."

She laughed. "Maybe that's the problem. I've forgotten what it's like to live a normal life."

"This too shall pass," he said reassuringly. "Don't worry about it. We'll deal with this and get you back to a normal work routine."

"Work?" She shook her head. "I have to find a damn job first."

"Not right now." He studied her face for a long moment as she watched him. Then he reached out a hand and gently stroked her cheek. "Did you hand in your resignation? Or did they fire you? You never did finish that part of the story."

"I couldn't stand it," she said quietly. "Always that sense of being watched, feeling I never had the freedom to do anything. After a particularly bad day, I gave my two weeks' notice. The last day I worked was Thursday."

"So you didn't work those two weeks?"

She shook her head. "I had six days of holidays coming, but I didn't actually tell them that. I was getting really scared, so I just took the second week off. And I quickly packed and moved out any personal stuff and was done," she said. "When I first found the information, I realized I would have to do something about it eventually. So I gave up the lease on my apartment and moved into a tiny studio for the last couple months. I gave away all my furniture as the studio came furnished." She shook her head. "Who knew I would have thought so far ahead? The thing is, I did it without thinking."

"It's called instinct," he said. "The company would've had your old address." He narrowed his gaze at her and added, "And may have accessed any forwarding info you shared with the post office. Unless you told somebody. Did you?"

She shook her head. "No, I didn't. I put an ad in the newspaper to sell the furniture but in the end just gave it all away. It was years old anyway. I never had much to begin with," she confessed. "So when I moved out of the studio, I could pack everything in my car. When I left, I still had another week's lease on the studio. Another reason for the timing of giving notice at work, but it's not like I'll go back and sleep there anymore."

"It's better not to go back, just in case somebody had been following you and knew where you had moved."

She felt a little ill at that thought. "In that case, maybe

my landlord's in trouble. He's a senior and lives above the small apartment," she said. "I don't want anything to happen to him."

"Give me his name and address. I'll see if any police reports or anything have been filed. There's probably been nothing, but I don't want him—or you—to worry unnecessarily."

She thought about that and then nodded. "Honestly I didn't feel like I was being followed to and from there, but … his name is Ryan Brown." She rattled off the address.

"Give me a second to phone the police station and confirm nothing has been reported." He stood up and walked to the other side of the room.

She called after him, "Can you just call and say, hey, I'm worried about somebody, and ask if there has been any incident?"

He turned to gaze at her and smiled. "I know several people in the local police department. A couple friends I went to school with. We can trust them to tell me of any problems in the area."

She wondered about that. Wouldn't it still trigger an interest? She couldn't quite decide if it was safe to make inquiries that led to other people's questions.

She sat there, trying to relax until he returned, marveling at the size of the place she was in. Windows were everywhere, but they were tinted, and she was sure some security system had been installed because barely visible wires were on the top of each window and door. She didn't know what Merk's group was all about, but the living room itself was the size of five normal living rooms with little gatherings of couch seating areas. She really liked it. She'd never been in a place quite so large.

This wasn't a traditional house. She could imagine twenty to thirty, even forty people staying here it was so big. Especially with the huge commercial kitchen area—definitely Alfred's domain.

The dining room itself could easily hold that many people. At the moment they had a huge long table, but then on the far side they had a bunch of smaller tables too. So space was not an issue. She'd really like to go for a walk out on the grounds but wasn't sure if that was okay or not. As soon as Merk got back, she might ask. Just something to help her relax before bed.

He returned a few minutes later. Instead of a smile on his face, the corners of his mouth were pinched, and his eyes were hard.

Instantly her heart froze, and her stomach heaved. "What happened?"

"The studio you lived in was broken into last night. The place was ripped to shreds."

"Oh, no. What about the landlord? Is Ryan okay?"

Merk nodded. "He called the police when he heard the ruckus going on, but, by the time they arrived, nobody was there. And, yes, he does have insurance to help cover the damage, but he's obviously upset."

"You think?" She shook her head. "So even though I was so careful, they still knew." She stared out into the evening sun and said quietly, "Dear God. What if I hadn't left?"

MERK HAD A little more to the report that Jonas had given him, but she didn't need to hear the details. The old man was safe and sound, and the police had been there and were working on the assumption that somebody was just angry.

Katina had actually absconded out from under their noses, and they were pissed. He patted her shoulder and said, "I'm heading over to talk to Levi and Ice about this development. You stay here. I'll be back in a few minutes. If you want to, maybe we could take a walk around the complex, or I can show you around the house."

When she nodded and sank back into the couch, he gave her a smile and headed to the office. He didn't know if Levi and Ice were in the control room or the office; he hoped they were off the phone so they could all match up their data at the moment.

In the office he found Levi writing notes, setting up a large whiteboard with what he knew. Merk stood in the doorway, glancing behind to ensure he was alone, then stepped in and closed the door. "Levi, there's been a development."

Levi turned, studied him, then asked, "What's up?"

He proceeded to tell him that Katina's place had been trashed, ending with, "Threats were written all over the walls too. Things like, *Bitch, we'll find you*, and *Where is it?*"

"What were the threats written in?"

Merk shrugged. "Didn't ask."

"Doesn't matter." Levi picked up his pen. "Either way they got the message across."

"Did you get a hold of Gunner?" Merk asked. "Is he okay if we see him tomorrow?"

"Hell, that man is excited already. He's delighted to be asked and overjoyed to help. He's really looking forward to being part of the action." Levi laughed. "I told him it was just documentation to be copied and dispersed, and he was like, *Best kind. Clandestine. I miss that.*"

At that, Merk had to laugh as well. "Too bad he had to

retire. That old man's got a lot of juice left in him."

Levi stopped, sat behind his desk, and studied Merk. "I'm actually wondering, since I got off the phone, if we could use him. He has a hell of a lot of information and skills. I just don't know to what extent those skills can be of help to us now."

"Depends on how many connections he maintains," Merk said. "If he's still in touch with those in the industry, then he's a huge resource. His intel would be massive for us."

Levi nodded. "Check him out while you're there. See just how interested he may be in doing some fact-checking," Levi said with a grin.

Merk knew perfectly well *fact-checking* meant *gathering intel.* "I think that's a good idea. We know and trust him, and he knows and trusts us, so ..."

Silence settled between the two of them for a long moment, then Levi said, "How attached are you to your ex-wife?"

"Not sure how to answer that. I was barely attached to her when she was my wife," he said with a grin. "We were literally together overnight. She flew out early the next afternoon, after we'd done necessary paperwork. We were married for all of a handshake when you look at it compared to the rest of our lives." He laughed. "Actually we've spent more time together this time around than we did when we got married."

"And how do you feel about it this time?" Levi's gaze narrowed as he studied Merk's face.

Merk sat down on the corner of the desk. "I'm not sure. Intrigued. Interested. Worried. It's all happened so fast I'm not exactly sure what to say."

"Like when you first met her."

"Absolutely. Only there's more to it now. She's tougher than she was then, and I like the woman she's become." He kept his face open and honest. He'd been friends with Levi for a long time. Merk knew the man was sorting something out, but he didn't know what. "What's really bothering you here?"

Levi heaved a sigh, stretched back in his chair with his hands behind his head, and kicked his feet up on the desk. "Just that we have a pattern setting in here. Look at Stone. He meets Lissa, moved her here to protect her, and she stays. Ice meets Sienna and decides to help her. Don't know about you, but I've certainly noticed the attraction between her and Rhodes no matter how much they try to ignore it."

"Oh, I've noticed," Merk said with a grin. "Now you're thinking how I get a call from Katina, needing my help. I moved her in to protect her." He tilted his head to the side. "And you're afraid she'll stay."

Levi's boots hit the floor as he leaned forward with a big laugh. "I'm not afraid of it. I just see it happening. I'm wondering if you do as well." He crossed his hands on the desk and said, "Has Terkel said anything to you about it?"

"No." Merk frowned. "In fact I haven't heard from him in a couple days. Of course Katina just contacted me." He turned to stare out the window. "Sometimes I worry about my brother."

"And so you should. The man who sees more than he should and tries to help everyone he can is destined for trouble," Levi said quietly. "I'd love to get his take on this. I wasn't planning on Legendary Security becoming a match-making service or to have our nickname, Heroes for Hire, which is bad enough, becoming Heroes of the Heart."

"They call, say they need help, so we move them in."

Merk laughed as he stood up. "The good thing about it is, it's a big place, boss. Sounds like we need more apartments finished." And he walked out, laughing.

But inside, the reminder of his brother not calling was worrisome. Not that they talked every day or every week; sometimes they went months without a word. Usually when something happened in Merk's life, Terkel knew. And he always called, sometimes with advice, sometimes with one of those little notes that came from having sensed something, and sometimes it was just that good old brotherly warning.

The fact that he hadn't contacted Merk was odd, what with Katina back in his life. He pulled out his phone, glancing down at it. He should call Terkel. Without questioning himself, he pulled up his brother's number and hit Dial as he wandered down the hall. He'd spent far too many years with Levi, was thinking like him.

With his phone to his ear, ringing and ringing endlessly, he found Katina curled up in the corner of the couch, sound asleep. When his brother's number finally went to his voice mail, Merk left a quick message and put away his phone.

He walked to the sideboard, opened the bottom drawer, pulled out a blanket, and returned to cover her up. He stood over her and wondered. She couldn't sleep very well in that crumpled position. Should he wake her or should he carry her to her bed?

As he stood, frowning down at her, she opened her eyes, saw him, and screamed.

Chapter 8

W ITH HER SCREAM reverberating throughout the room, Katina struggled to get free of whatever was wrapped around her. Suddenly somebody snatched her up, and a familiar voice whispered in her ear, "Easy, Katina. Take it easy. It's just me, Merk."

Instantly she stopped struggling but lay shuddering in his arms, her gaze locked onto his face as the truth settled in. It really was him. She buried her face against his chest, but she couldn't stop the shivers that wracked down her spine.

He sat down on the couch with her, holding her close.

Footsteps raced into the room. Levi and Ice both stopped at the entranceway, and Levi asked, "What's wrong?"

"Is she okay?" Rhodes asked from the other end of the room with Alfred.

"It's okay. I covered her up with a blanket. She woke up, saw me, and screamed."

Katina, her face red with humiliation, said, "I'm so sorry, everyone. I didn't mean to panic like that."

Stone snorted from the side by the kitchen. "Who could blame you? If I woke up with that looming over me, I'd be screaming like a girl too." He gave her a wink and walked from the room.

Alfred said, "I'll bring a pot of tea to calm her down

some." And he rushed away.

Merk glanced at Levi, gave a tiny shrug and a smile.

But Katina noticed. She glanced at the two of them and apologized again. "I am sorry."

In a bright voice Ice said, "Don't apologize. There's no need. You've been to hell and back. That you haven't fallen apart before now is already admirable. When you sleep, the subconscious does all kinds of horrible things. Don't worry about it. It's all good." She nudged Levi in the shoulder and said, "Come on back to the office. Stuff you need to deal with."

Feeling better but still embarrassed, Katina sank back into Merk's arms, only to realize where she was. She struggled to sit up. "I can sit on the couch."

But his arms tightened around her, and he said, "You could sit on the couch, but I really don't want you to. You scared me," he complained. "I need to hold you to know you're okay."

She snorted. "Does that line really work for you?"

He glanced down at her with a wicked grin and said, "It must. You're in my arms still."

She leaned back to gasp in his face. And then laughed. "You're incorrigible."

He tucked her up close again and kissed her lightly on the temple. "As long as you're okay, then I'm fine."

She let herself relax into the warmth of his chest. After a few minutes of just resting, she said in a small voice, "Did you think about me ever?"

Lying against him as she was, in no way could she could miss the surprised start of his body. But he didn't stiffen in outrage, and she knew whatever answer came would likely be the truth.

"A few times," he admitted. "We didn't have much time together, but the time we did have was … incredible."

Once again she tilted her head back so she could see his face. "It was, wasn't it?" She beamed up at him. "Nice to know we got something right back then."

He chuckled. "We were both very young. Both of us had plans for our lives. And it didn't include getting married to a stranger. We had a good time. We did what we did. Afterward we fixed it, and we moved on."

"Yep," she said with a comical tone. "And then I called you for help." She shook her head. "Who does that?"

"And why me?"

"I don't know," she said. "Honestly I didn't think the number would work."

"I kept your number all these years," he admitted. He pulled out his phone and checked his contacts. Sure enough there, way down at the bottom under Marshal, was Katina's name and number. He turned to look at her and said, "I honestly don't remember getting your phone number back then."

"Oh, I do. At brunch the next day—when we were exchanging information so we could get a divorce," she said in a dry tone. "I called you several times this week." She reached out and slugged him lightly on the chest. "But you never answered."

"I was off on a job when you first called," he admitted. "Depending on the type of mission, I leave my personal cell phone at home. We have a special one for the unit as we go out on jobs."

That made sense. She sank back and said, "Thanks for answering my call."

"Even then we didn't meet up as intended. I was inside

the damn restaurant waiting for you."

At that, she sat up straight and said, "What I said was, meet me at noon. So you mean, you were inside having lunch and a beer while I was standing outside waiting for you?"

"You said noon, but you didn't say outside in the parking lot. I automatically assumed it would be inside, where it was nice and comfortable. We'd have lunch, and you'd explain whatever problem you had." He shifted her slightly so she was in a better position on his lap, then added, "I wasn't expecting to see you picked up and tossed into a vehicle in front of me and carted away."

"Yeah, isn't that the truth." She yawned, quickly covering her mouth as she did so. "Sorry. I guess I'm still tired."

Just then Alfred walked in with a tray. She glanced at his face and said in a heartfelt voice, "Thank you, Alfred. You are such a gem to treat me so nicely."

He patted her gently and said, "You need a little bit of loving care right now, so a cup of tea is a perfect way to just let the world fade away."

She glanced at the tray, realizing that the loving cup of tea came with a plateful of treats. As soon as she saw the food, she realized she was hungry. She scrambled off Merk's lap to sit beside him, picked up a slice of something that looked like banana bread. She broke off a piece and popped it in her mouth. "Oh, my God! This is so good."

"Alfred, this is a hell of a deal." Merk reached across and grabbed a slice of the second type of bread on the plate. "I think he's on a secret mission to fatten us all up," Merk said in a conspiratorial voice. "We're all very willing victims of his conspiracy."

She grinned. "While that's a good thing, if you can't eat

your share of this, I'll eat it for you."

"Not happening." As if to make sure, he broke off a piece of the treat she was eating.

As he sat back in comfortable silence, each enjoying their snack, she remembered where he had headed off to before she'd zonked out. "You went to talk to Levi. What was the end result of that?"

He shrugged. "A lot. We'll go to Gunner's house early tomorrow morning." He slid a glance her way and said, "After we pick up the key."

She didn't answer for a moment, then said, "Okay. That works. As long as you trust Gunner."

"With the type work we do, trusting the wrong people can get us killed. We trust very few, but, of those we do, we trust them implicitly."

AFTER FINISHING THEIR snack, he could see her eyes drooping. He stood up, held out a hand. "Come on. Let's get you to your room. You're almost asleep now. You'd sleep better after a shower."

"I would love a shower," she admitted. "Being tossed around on the floor in the van wasn't exactly a nice experience." She stood up. "Not to mention my bloodied leg. Nothing a good night's sleep won't fix," she said in a determined voice.

He led the way to the stairs, then changed his mind and went across to the elevator on the far side. "Shouldn't put any more stress on that leg."

He sent the elevator up to the second floor and led her down the hallway to the bedroom Ice had set up for her. When he unlocked the door and helped her back in, he pointed to her bags stacked on the side and said, "There's your stuff. If you want a shower, go for it. The bathroom is through that small door there." He paused and then said, "Call me if you need me. I'll come. I'm on the same floor but down the other side."

She nodded. "Thanks. I'm sure I'll be fine." She turned to close the door behind him, whispering, "Good night."

He stood outside, waiting to hear the *click* of the lock. But she didn't lock it. He frowned. She needed to get used to locking doors. A good habit to get into. Although she was safe here tonight.

He walked back to the office to see Ice and Levi discussing the budget and manpower allocation, picked up a chair, brought it nearer to them, and said, "Has this to do with tomorrow, or is it just me taking her to Gunner's?"

When Levi shook his head, Merk nodded. "Who's running backup then?"

Levi said, "I think both Ice and I will go in. We'll stay back to observe if anybody else catches sight of you. Plus we want to talk to Gunner."

Ice turned toward Merk and asked, "Has she given any indication where the key is?"

Merk shook his head. "No, but every time I mention it, she gets really quiet. I'm still not sure what the deal is, but she said she'll take us there tomorrow." He reached up and ran his fingers through his hair. "Whatever that means. Honestly I'm not sure, but something odd is going on."

"Do you trust her?" Levi asked. "It's not a good time for something odd to be going on."

"I know," Merk said. He glanced around the room and said, "It's quite possible she might actually have it on her and doesn't want to let us know. Not until we're ready to go."

"But then we would be better off dealing with it here," Ice said. "We can have the copies taken care of with our equipment and send it out through our secure system."

"I told her that, but she's not buying it."

The three exchanged glances.

"We didn't ask to search her luggage, and, of course, we didn't take that opportunity when we had it."

"No, wouldn't want to either," Merk said firmly. "She asked us for help. That she hasn't handed the key over already means she doesn't trust us. So it's up to us to encourage her."

But inside he worried too. He had no idea if she was telling the truth about even having the information. And his friends had gone out on a limb to help her. He wanted her to be on the up-and-up, but was she? What did he really know about her? Like he'd said, trust was hard.

"I really hope she doesn't turned around and trip us up with this." And then, because he just couldn't keep that thought to himself, he said, "I can't see any reason for her to do so, but ..."

"Unless she tries to run in the morning."

Merk stared at Ice and frowned. He considered the fact that the gates were locked and that Katina knew she couldn't get out.

"What she could do, when the gates are open, is make a mad dash for her car and run," Ice suggested.

"Even then we can't take it in a negative way," Merk said calmly. "Because, for all we know, she's hidden it in the car." He stood up. "Nothing more we can really do until morning. I'll call it a night then." He turned and walked out.

He didn't know what tomorrow would bring, but, as he'd originally planned to walk past her bedroom and make sure she was all right, he deliberately forced himself to go in the opposite direction. There was just too much uncertainty right now.

He'd been betrayed once on the job. Hell, they all had. The physical fallout had been brutal. Just look at Stone's missing leg. But that wasn't the same thing as betrayal by a lover, ... yet learning to trust was hard. Still, someone must take a leap of faith here. He only had the little insight he knew of the girl from over a decade ago. But she'd been real, authentic back then. So what had the intervening years done for—to—her?

Chapter 9

W HEN SHE OPENED her eyes the next morning, it was
to a heavy heart and a weird groggy sensation. She
understood what was happening today but still worried it
wasn't the right thing to do. A part of her felt she should just
run, get the hell out of Dodge. Forget about the USB stick.
But she wasn't sure she could outrun her past. And did she
really want to look over her shoulder forever?

Neither did she want to let go of that tenuous relationship she'd found again with Merk. She could've given them
the key already. They could've taken care of everything in
their office here.

But what if someone had followed her, was here already?
For the same damn reason she was concerned about going to
this Gunner's place. Particularly if the bad guys followed
them to his house.

She just didn't know enough, and that scared her. She'd
been so exhausted last night that she had collapsed into bed
without a shower, but now she was feeling dirty and desperately in need of something to wake her up. And to loosen the
tight hold on her chest. Her leg was sore but not painful.
More of a dull ache that just bloomed inside her.

She headed to the bathroom, turned on the shower, and
stripped out of her underwear and T-shirt. She stepped into
the warm water and let the spray take away some of her pain.

She was so lost and at a crossroads right now. She had no job, no home. She had her vehicle but was living off the generosity of Merk.

Which reminded her a lot of her childhood. She'd been permanently caught between families and yet belonged to none. Now it seemed as if nothing had changed, and she was still repeating childish patterns of existence.

What the hell did that say about her? This was not where she had expected to be. She'd had such high hopes when she went to Vegas. Eleven years later, it seemed she'd gotten nowhere. During all that time she'd kept quiet about her marriage. She'd told Anna but no one else. Then Anna had been in Vegas with Katina. She'd graduated, done all the normal things, but she had never found another relationship quite like the short one she had had with Merk. Maybe she didn't trust herself anymore.

She'd had relationships; she'd had lovers, but nothing went the distance. And yet, as soon as she saw Merk again, the same damn attraction lit up her insides like a firecracker. They'd been combustible back then, and she already knew it would be very difficult to stop that same fuse from blowing up this time too. He was lethal. He was also a hell of a lover, and she knew that, with the passage of those eleven years and a lot more experience under his belt, he'd be just as lethal, if not more so.

She turned off the shower and reached for two towels, one for her hair, then carefully dried herself off and took a good look at her leg. Clean, it didn't look so bad. The bandage had come off in the shower, and she didn't have another one to put on. No way could she wear pants over her wound without the stitches catching every few minutes.

Katina frowned. What were her options? Shorts? She

glanced outside and realized it was hardly shorts weather.

With her bags open, she studied her clothing. She really didn't want to wear a skirt either. She had a couple, but they weren't practical if things went down the shitter.

So shorts it was. At least until she could ask for another bandage. She unwrapped the towel from her head, quickly dressed, brushed her hair, and braided her long rich locks. She tossed the braid down the center of her back and efficiently packed up the last of her clothing. She left out a pair of jeans to change into.

Quickly glancing around the bathroom to ensure it was clean and she'd left nothing behind, she made her way to the door. It was still early, but she suspected it wasn't early for this household. She opened the door and found the hallway empty. She knew her way at least to the stairs.

She slowly worked her way down the risers, happy her leg was a lot more flexible and her joints moved easily. Her body was pretty bruised and achy after the van ride, but, all in all, today was a whole new day. Maybe, with any luck, she could get rid of this burden she'd been carrying. As long as nobody else got hurt, she was fine with that.

The main floor was empty, but she could smell coffee. She followed the aroma and found Stone sitting at the main table with Lissa. She smiled at the two of them and said, "Good morning, I smell coffee."

Stone nodded his massive head and said, "Yep, that's the one standard around here." He pointed to the sidebar where the coffeepot sat.

She grabbed one of the cups sitting on a tray and poured herself a cup, then turned to the couple and asked, "Is it okay if I sit here?"

Lissa jumped to her feet and said, "Oh, my goodness, of

course, sit down. It's all really very casual around this place."

"I figured as much. Just hadn't quite sorted out how everything worked yet."

"The team lives here, and those of us who are partners live here with them," Lissa said cheerfully. "Stone and I just moved into one of the apartments on the far side, but we haven't got our place organized yet, so we're still effectively living in the main building." She patted Stone's big hand and said, "Hopefully this weekend we can get that all done." She laced her fingers with his and continued, "Not sure it will change much though. We're still over here for every meal."

Katina looked at her and asked, "Why is that?"

Lissa laughed. "I can't cook. Other than just the very basics. And Alfred here will be heartbroken if he has two less people to cook for."

"Actually that I can believe. I think Alfred is someone who likes to feed the world and be surrounded by lots of family."

Hearing voices, she looked up to see the rest of the crew in various states of wakefulness grabbing coffee. The men appeared to be relatively alert. She expected, with their jobs, that they had really little choice. They were all expected to get up and go at any given moment.

She sat quietly watching everybody in their natural setting. It was a unique way to see these people. Merk said they were a private security company, all ex-military, and she had a pretty good idea that the term "private security" was just a euphemism for doing whatever the hell the world needed them to do.

Finally Merk walked in, his gaze checking out the table before landing on her. Instantly his shoulders eased, and she realized he'd probably gone to her room looking for her. She gave him a crooked smile and said, "See? I didn't run away in the night."

He shrugged. "There's no place you could run to." He poured coffee and sat down beside her. Glancing at her bare legs, he raised one eyebrow and said, "Not sure it's a shorts kind of day."

She laughed. "It's Texas. Isn't it always shorts weather here? However, my bandage came off in the shower. Anybody have a medical kit handy? I need another bandage to cover the wound," she said, glancing down at her leg admitting, "I wasn't looking forward to putting on jeans and having the stitches rub."

Ice spoke up from the far end of the table. "You want to do it now or wait until after breakfast?"

Just then Alfred walked in with a great big platter of sausages, bacon, fresh bread, and a big bowl of scrambled eggs.

Katina raised her head to sniff in appreciation. "Oh, after breakfast for sure."

Everybody laughed and settled into eating.

When she was done, Ice led her down another floor into what appeared to be a full medical clinic.

Katina walked into the room in amazement. "This is something else." She noted several hospital beds. "Are you equipped to do surgery here?"

Ice laughed. "We've certainly done several, but, if it's major, we go to the hospital." She motioned to Katina's leg. "That, however, is something I can handle." She patted one of the beds and said, "Hop up so I can take a look at what size bandage we need."

Carefully Katina stretched her leg out so Ice could get at it. She brought over a couple bandages and found one that was about the right size.

"This should last you for the day. Let me know tonight, and we can change it out after a bath or shower again, if you want."

Katina didn't say anything. She wasn't expecting to be here tonight. These people had done more than enough to keep her safe, but she didn't want to trespass on their generosity. When Ice was done, Katina murmured, "Thank you. Much appreciated."

After that she went up to her room and quickly changed into jeans. She packed up her shorts and carried her bags out to the hallway. She had so many that it would take several trips to get them all in her car again.

As she picked up several, Merk joined her. "Just leave them here for now," he said in a firm voice. "You can decide what you want to do after we deal with the issues today."

She stared at him and chewed on her bottom lip. "I don't want to stay here another night," she explained. "You've done enough already."

He snorted. "Don't even start with me." He picked up her bags, took them inside her room, then shut the door behind her. "Let's go. We're taking my truck."

She was afraid of that. It meant she couldn't run away while in town. The fact of the matter was, he was right. She had no place to run to. So no point in arguing.

He led the way to the truck. She climbed into the passenger side, her purse at her side, and waved at the others on the driveway. Merk pulled out of the compound and headed through the gates. At the road, he stopped and said, "Which way, left or right?"

She turned to look at him. Of course, the USB key. He had no idea where it was.

She said quietly, "Right."

He put on a signal and turned right. For better or for worse she was committed now. No way would he let her get away without handing over the information.

Maybe it was for the best. Something had to be done. And she couldn't do it alone.

IT FASCINATED HIM to watch her facial expressions as her thought processes worked. Still uncertain of him, yet worried for him.

He clenched the steering wheel a little tighter as he let go of some of his anger. She had no good reason to trust him. She didn't really know him. They had had a fling a long time ago, and that was it. This was a life-and-death situation for her, already evident by her kidnapping. But surely she had to understand she needed help to handle this.

He followed her directions and came to one of the main banks. Then he realized she'd probably hid it in a safety deposit box. It made him feel a whole lot better. Not in her purse after all. He hopped out, walked around to open the truck door, and helped her down. Inside she asked the teller to get in her safety deposit box.

The woman nodded, and, within minutes, they were inside the small room with the box in front of them. The bank employee left.

With a glance at Merk, Katina opened the box and pulled out what looked like a child's souvenir. Then he realized it was a cheap souvenir key chain from Las Vegas.

He watched her carefully, wondering why she would've hung on to something like that all these years, or had she gone back recently? Oddly enough the thought hurt that she may have returned to Las Vegas without him. And that was just ridiculous.

She pulled apart the souvenir, and he could see it was a USB drive as well as a key chain. He nodded. "Good. Let's go."

She closed the box and left the room with a smile at the employee.

Back outside he wondered at her slow footsteps. As he got back into the truck, he said, "Are you still bothered about handing the information over?"

She gave him a shuttered look and then said, "I guess. Will you be upset that this is only part of it?"

He froze. Instead of turning on the engine, he slowly dropped his hand on the seat beside him and turned to look at her. "What do you mean?"

She stared down at the cheap plastic item in her hand and said, "I only had time to copy part of it."

"So you don't have all the evidence you were talking about?"

Again that same look came his way. "I do, just not in this form."

He slowly let out his breath, realizing he was clenching his jaw. He understood fear held her back, and he had to be patient. But, at the same time, he was frustrated as hell, needing reassurance of something else. "You're not playing games with me, are you?"

She shook her head. "No."

"Do we have to pick up anything else up in order to have all the information?"

"No." She opened her mouth as if to say something else, then closed it again.

He shook his head. She was damn infuriating.

He pulled from the parking lot with a quick glance to double-check they weren't being followed. Traffic was light. They arrived at Gunner's house in just under fifteen minutes. A trip made almost in complete silence.

What had she meant? Not only was she silent but she was curled up in the corner of the truck, like she wanted to be anywhere else. Too damn bad. This had gone way too far to stop the train now. Having the USB key was only part of it. The damaging information had to be intact as well.

At Gunner's they got out and walked up to the front door. It opened automatically in front of them. She looked at Merk in surprise.

He shrugged. "Gunner's into security. The door wouldn't have opened if he didn't know who was here."

They stepped inside the entranceway to stand on the huge hardwood floor, and there was Gunner, a big smile on his face.

"Well, look who is here."

Merk shot out a hand to shake his. The two exchanged greetings. Gunner had always been one of the white-hat guys. That was a good thing. Little enough of that in this world.

Gunner gently reached out to greet Katina. "Hello, my dear. I hear you got yourself in a spot of trouble."

That startled a hiccup of a laugh out of Katina. "You could say that," she whispered. "It's really not where I expected to see myself."

He motioned them inside and said, "Life is like that. Levi and Ice will be here any minute. I'm so happy to see you all."

They waited until Levi and Ice walked into the entranceway, both looking cool and composed. They were a power couple in their world. Interestingly enough, Merk could sense more nerves coming over Katina as their numbers doubled. He caught Ice's questioning look. He shrugged. He had no clue what was going on.

Gunner said, "I understand we have a bit of work to do. I'll arrange for coffee." He walked into a large office where his assistant sat. "You can give the key to him. He'll bring up the data, and we can take a look at what you've got."

Katina froze. In fact, she took a step back. Merk instantly wrapped an arm around her shoulder and whispered in her ear, "What's up?"

"I don't know him," she whispered. She winced. "It's stupid, but I'm struggling to hand it over."

Merk studied the assistant. He knew the man, and he was looking quite uncomfortable at the obvious attention.

Merk turned to Gunner and asked, "Do you mind if I handle this?"

Gunner waved his hand. "Go for it. I trust you won't access anything else in my computers that you don't need to."

"Your man can stand and watch. I don't mind that."

Merk sat down and held out his hand for the key. Without questioning, Katina handed over the trinket. He opened it up and popped the USB into the drive. There were three files. He opened the first one, and, as she said, it was spreadsheets of accounts.

Everybody moved to study the monitors. The assistant leaned down and switched a couple things, and then the spreadsheets opened onto the monitors higher up. That way they could take a closer look at the information. Merk moved the first file to one monitor, and then, with the assistant's help, he opened up the other two files so they could see the three files at the same time.

Behind him Ice commented, "Interesting."

Merk turned to look at Katina. "And where's the rest of the information?" He felt both Ice and Levi stare at him.

She flushed. "I have it," she said. She looked over at Gunner and then at his assistant, and said, "Do you happen to have a laptop with a mike attached?"

Gunner picked up a nearby laptop and brought it to her while the assistant grabbed one of several headsets sitting on the shelf. Quietly she hooked everything up.

She pulled up a chair to the desk and spoke into the machine. She relaxed in the chair, and the words just rolled off the tip of her tongue. She closed her eyes and settled in.

Merk stared at her in shock. He stood behind her to see the words as they rippled onto the notepad. And then he realized what she had meant. She couldn't download a lot of files without triggering the wrong kind of attention, so she'd memorized the contents. He shook his head, watching as the information floated almost magically onto the page. Beside him, Ice and Levi just stared. Merk knew how they felt.

Gunner stood beside him. "You know, this looks like it might take a while. Time for that coffee." And he left the room.

No way would Merk interrupt Katina at this point. But now he realized why she'd been so secretive. This wasn't something she wanted anybody to know she could do. Hell, it was quite a skill, but it wasn't one he'd want the bad guys to know about either. What methods they would use to force her to get info—or, even worse, to forcefully get data from her—would be horrific.

He pulled up a chair and sat down, reading the information as it went. After forty-five minutes of steady dictation, she stopped suddenly, sat taller, opened a spreadsheet, and verbally filled in the tables from memory. Merk looked at Ice and Levi. Both frowned at the shift.

Ice said, "You must have been dynamite in school."

"Hell, she'd be dynamite in any team." Merk wondered how the hell she could do this.

Finally she fell silent. He checked his watch and realized she'd been speaking steadily for over ninety minutes. He shook his head. He reached for a glass of water on the tray being wheeled in and handed it to her. With a grateful smile she drank the whole glass at once.

"Do you want more?" he asked.

She shook her head. "I should be fine now."

"Besides that magical display of whatever it was you just did," Merk said quietly, "is there any other information you haven't given us?"

She shook her head. "No. That's all I have."

Chapter 10

WITH A CUP of coffee in her hand, and her work done, she relaxed. Now that she finally got it all out, a sense of relief came as she had finally committed to a pathway—good or bad. Whenever she had to do something like this, it always terrified her that she'd miss some information. Forget it before she had a chance to write it down. But she knew this time she'd gotten it all.

She could see the look on their faces as they read the information she'd poured out. Somebody should transcribe it to correct the errors inherent in any dictation program. She made a couple corrections, but, as far as she was concerned, the information was complete. Between what she got on the key and what she remembered, it should be enough. At least enough for the police to go on.

And now she was tired. Which was stupid because it was not even lunchtime. She felt like she'd been through the ringer and back.

She sat quietly while the others discussed the information. Gunner's assistant was already going through it, cleaning it up and making it more legible. She watched, making sure he didn't change anything important. It wouldn't take too long, she knew from experience. When he finally finished, he sent it to the printer and gave them each a hard copy to read over. She didn't accept the one he handed her way. She knew what it said. The last thing she wanted to do was go over it again.

"So why is there a file with all these names of places and money? I understand what you say now about a code and the word *cop* beside three of them. It's not much of a name to go on, but surely we can get somewhere with this."

"That was the accountant's private file," Katina said quietly. "All kinds of restrictions were on that copy. I couldn't print it. It wouldn't let me do anything. The accountant was the only one who could edit it in any way. The only thing I could do was memorize it."

"You can use programs to take copies of stuff like that on screens."

She nodded. "But they also keep copies of what you've taken copies of," she murmured. "And I couldn't afford to let anybody know what I was doing."

Gunner stepped in and said, "But obviously somebody does if you were kidnapped, dear."

She grimaced. "Yes, but at the time I didn't think anyone knew."

He nodded in understanding and said, "Write down all who should get copies of this."

And that settled into a heavy discussion of names, options, emails, and contacts. They all elected to go with duplicate mailings, both print and digital, just in case. Ten names were finally settled upon.

To her that was a lot. Hesitantly, when they were finally done, she said, "Are you sure all these people are trustworthy?"

"No being sure about any of it," Gunner said in his best military voice. "All we can do is assume that people we have known and worked with and have witnessed how they acted in various situations are on the side of right."

"In other words it's a crapshoot ..."

Merk laughed. "Back to Vegas again, are we?"

At that moment, the assistant removed the key, popped the cover on, and handed her the trashy Vegas trinket.

Merk looked at her and smiled. "It seems like things come full circle."

She dropped it into her purse and zipped it up. She glanced at the assistant and smiled, saying, "Thank you."

He nodded but was already back at work. The spreadsheets were printing off right now. Ten copies. She looked back at the list of names and said, "Are any of these people media?"

"One is a journalist of high repute," Gunnar said. "He's well-known as a whistleblower."

She nodded. "If it's as good as we can do, then I leave the names in your hands."

"And that," Ice said with a smile, "is why you called Merk in the first place, so relax. This is what we do."

Before Katina had a chance to answer, Merk reached across and picked up her hand, holding it gently in his. "It will be fine."

"Really? I'm pretty damn sure that's what you said before you led me into the Elvis Presley Wedding Chapel."

The entire group burst out laughing. That was good because she'd rather laugh than cry and that was her only other option at the moment.

"Photographic memory?" Merk asked quietly at her side.

She turned to look at him and nodded. Then shrugged. "Or maybe not. It's something like that but not quite. I never asked anyone."

His intense gaze locked on hers as if he was seeing if she

had more secrets hidden away. She let him look all he wanted. She knew she'd been emptied right out, and the process had exhausted her.

She closed her eyes and just rested.

"How come I didn't know about this before?" he complained in a lighthearted manner.

Without opening her eyes, she said, "You weren't too interested in *what* was inside me. More interested in getting inside me," she said in a very low voice. But, at the sudden silence in the room, she knew everybody had heard. Feeling the heat wash up her face, she whispered, "Damn. No one else was supposed to hear that."

Beside her, Levi snickered. "At least you understand Merk very clearly."

"Hey, that's not fair," Merk said with a grin. "I was very much interested in a lot more than that." But the humor ramped up in his voice as he added, "Although I was definitely concerned about that part."

She laughed. "I have to admit that's one thing we did a lot of. Laugh." She'd already brought up more sexual innuendos than she had expected to. Apparently this was who she was with him. They had laughed and joked and had a grand time. But the experience had also soured and scared her. She still considered tequila one of the devil's best tricks.

The topic returned to the information and all the names. "Can I leave now?" she asked, fatigue getting the best of her.

All heads turned, and everyone zeroed in on her. But Merk voiced the unasked question, "Go where?"

"Anywhere. How about California?" she asked mockingly. "I have an uncle in Canada. Maybe I should go visit him."

"Do you want to run for the rest of your life?" Ice asked.

"That's no way to live. You'll always be looking over your shoulder. Is Canada far enough away? Maybe. Until some-body, somewhere, somehow finds out who you are, and it gets back to these people."

Katina frowned. "No, that's no kind of life, is it?" She looked around at the rest of them and added, "But all this is likely to do is make things bigger and uglier."

"In the short term, yes," Merk said. "I don't know what your financial situation is, but maybe a holiday isn't a bad idea. At least until this all blows over."

"Meaning Canada is possible?" She sat up, liking the idea. Her uncle was great. She'd love to spend a few weeks with him. "How different is that from running away to Canada then?" she joked.

"It's all about intention," Merk said. "One is staying low and getting out of the limelight until the kidnappers can be caught and brought to trial, and the other is not planning on heading anywhere in particular, running, hoping that you'll be free and always looking over your shoulder. One is planned. The other is not."

"I have handed over everything I know of," Katina said firmly. "Probably more information is in my brain if you can dredge it out of me. I really don't want to run away. But an extended holiday would be a nice idea. Only not to my uncle if that'll put him in danger."

"You don't trust your uncle?" Levi asked.

She turned to look at him. "As much as I trust any-body," she admitted, hating that trust appeared to be such an issue for her. She'd been alone most of her life. Independent by necessity and depending on others wasn't something she had experience in. "I don't think he has anything to do with this. But I don't want to bring any trouble to his doorstop either."

Levi nodded. "That's good to know."

Merk spoke from the other side of her, making her twist back to look at him. "Does anyone involved know about your uncle?" He nodded at all the spreadsheets in front of them.

She let out her breath, slowly thinking about what could be in her personnel file. "I don't think so, but I suppose, if they wanted to search deep enough, they would find that information somehow."

Gunner spoke up and said, "Absolutely they would." He waited a moment and then said, "But they'd have to think that's a place you would go. They won't go all around the world on a goose chase if they think you're close. Or if you have other addresses, other friends who might yield them better results."

Friends? *Anna.* Sitting up straighter, Katina turned cold, knowing the color had been leached from her skin. "Would they really go after my friends?"

Silence.

"You were already worried about the landlord living above you. How is it you haven't connected they might give any of your friends and family a shakedown to find out where you are?" Ice asked.

Shaking, Katina pulled her purse toward her from the side of the chair and dug for her phone. She brought up her contact list and hit the first one at the top. Her best friend worked in an animal shelter. When she answered the call, Katina sat back, relieved. "Anna, any chance you could disappear for a couple weeks?"

First came silence. And then Anna cried out, "What's wrong? Are you hurt? I heard about the kidnapping. You could have called to let me know you're okay. I've been so worried."

Katina lifted a hand to her forehead. "I'm so sorry. I was trying to keep you out of this. I didn't want anyone to track you down. Honestly my life's just been hell these last twenty-four hours. I haven't had time to think clearly."

"I've been so worried," Anna wailed. "Oh, my God, what's going on with you?"

Katina didn't know what to tell her friend.

"Katina," Anna continued in a sharp tone, "what's this about me leaving?"

"I got into a bit of trouble. I'm on the wrong side of a lot of people who are on the other side of the law, and they're after me," she said. "The people helping me are concerned that my friends—you—might be targets."

More silence then she said, "Oh, my God."

Katina winced. "I know. I know. I'm so sorry. And I understand this is sudden, but things are about to hit the fan here in the next twenty-four hours, and I want to make sure you're safe."

She could just imagine her friend standing in the middle of the shelter, looking at all the animals in need, knowing instinctively what she would say.

"I can't," Anna said. "You know I have almost no staff anymore. The shelter's struggling to stay afloat as it is. Somebody has to be here to look after these animals."

Her gaze zinged over toward Merk. "I know that, Anna, but I'd die if anything happened to you because of me."

"Are these the same guys who kidnapped you?"

"Likely, yes. Or the people who hired them."

"I have a security system here and at home," Anna said. "I can hardly just pack up and walk away. It's not that simple."

"I know." Katina sank back against the chair and wiped the tears forming in the corner of her eyes. "I know exactly how hard it is. Everything I own is in the back of my car. I've lost everything."

"It's that stupid accounting job when you got a promotion, right?"

Katina frowned into the phone. "How did you know that?" She sensed the interest coming from everybody around her. But she shook her head, holding them off.

"You changed after that. You got really nervous, kept looking over your shoulder. I asked if everything was okay, and you said it was fine. But I knew you were lying."

"It's not so much that I was lying. I kept looking over my shoulder, but nothing was ever there," she explained. "And then suddenly somebody was. And that's when I was kidnapped."

"Who are the people helping you?"

Katina hesitated.

"Don't lie. I have enough issues to deal with here. Exactly what the hell's going on? So who is helping you, and are they to be trusted?"

Knowing what was coming, she braced for the worst when she said, "I called Merk."

Anna snorted and said, "You're kidding me. You called your Las Vegas husband?" She had said it in such a loud voice, Katina was damn sure half the room heard her.

"Ex-husband," she said firmly. "Besides, he was going into the military, remember? I didn't know who else to call. I figured maybe he would know who could help me. I wasn't expecting him to insist on being the one to step up."

"Oh, that's too funny. Your Elvis Presley Wedding

Chapel experience turned into a white knight." And then she giggled.

Katina was pretty damn sure it was more of a release over the stress than anything, but Anna was enjoying herself a little too much.

Merk leaned across and tapped her on the knee. "Tell her you will call her back in a few minutes."

She nodded and quickly rang off the phone call. She put the phone in her lap and stared at him. "What?"

He looked over at Levi and said, "Do we have anyone who could go help out at the shelter and keep an eye on Anna?"

Levi frowned but turned to Ice, thinking. "All our full-time men are out on jobs."

"That's another thing," Ice said. "It could be several weeks to several months."

Merk nodded. "Gunner, what about you? It doesn't have to be a full-time cop or a security guard, but somebody with military training, somebody retired who is no longer in service for one reason or another."

Katina had no idea what that *one reason or other* would be.

"As long as they had good solid experience in looking after somebody and were okay to help out with the animals, it would be a win-win on both sides. She's completely short-staffed and is overwhelmed with animals."

"Speaking of someone good with animals"—Merk turned to look at Levi—"how is Aaron?"

Levi shook his head. "Not ready for that yet. Still has surgeries ahead of him for the leg and back."

Merk nodded. "Too bad. He'd be an ideal fit. He loves animals."

"Yeah, when he was a young man, before the military," Levi said. "From all accounts he's become very bitter and not dealing well with his changed circumstances." He frowned and dropped his gaze to the floor.

"There are many like him," Gunner said quietly. "Now the question is, who do I know who would be the right pick for the job?" He sat there and dropped his pencil up and down on the paper. "Let me think about that for a few minutes and see if I can come up with somebody."

With that, Katina was happy and hoped that some solution came up and soon. She'd be devastated if anything happened to Anna.

MERK WATCHED KATINA slip the phone around and around in her fingers as she fretted over the safety of her friend. "How many friends could be affected by this?"

She looked up at him in surprise. "Anna would be the closest and the most in danger. We did a lot of sleepovers. We were quite visibly friends since forever. Same schools and college. She's the reason I stayed in Houston. With no family to care about, Anna was closer to being my real sister than the two half-sisters I do have. It was an obvious choice to stay here. As good a location as any." She flushed. "Actually Anna was in Vegas too. And the only one who knows what I was doing there."

Merk frowned. "I didn't see her."

She gave him a pointed look and said, "No, you were looking at something else."

He grinned. "I have good taste."

She shook her head and rolled her eyes at him. Although this was the last thing she'd expected to be joking about, it really did help ease the tension in the room.

"I do have other friends, but they don't live in town, and I don't know how much danger they would be in. I guess somebody could go to them and ask about me, but I haven't discussed this with anyone. Honestly I wasn't terribly social at work either." And then her voice fell away. She pinched her brows together deep in thought.

Merk gave her a minute and then asked, "What are you thinking about?"

She chewed the inside her lip and said, "It can't be."

"What can't be?" Ice asked. "Better let us decide."

Katina stared down at her hands and how she continuously flipped her phone around in her lap. "Another woman worked for us. She replaced a different accountant but just temporarily because he was attending a conference." She shrugged. "But I don't know why they would replace anybody for that week. The job normally would have been off-loaded to another one of the senior accountants or just left until they got back."

"And?" Merk asked. "There has to be more to this if it's bothering you."

"It wasn't bothering me until just now, when I realized that she disappeared."

Instantly everyone in the room sat up and stared at her. "Okay, I don't mean 'disappeared.' She left the building one day, and the next day I noticed her coat was still there, as if she'd rushed out and never wanted to come back to collect it."

"Or is it that she couldn't come back?" Merk said quietly.

She stared at him open-mouthed, her eyes round as saucers, and she cried, "Oh, no, there's no reason for them to do something like that, is there, Merk?"

"Hard to say. What was her name?" Gunner asked.

"Eloise Hartman."

"When did she disappear?"

Katina frowned, thinking. "Middle of March, I think," she said. "I was already in the new position, but I had only been there a couple days. She made some comment about me having fun, but her tone wasn't normal. Not snide and it wasn't offered as a warning, but something was just off about it."

Merk watched Gunner tap on his laptop, searching for Eloise Hartman. He studied Gunner's face as it changed. And then he knew. "What? A drive-by shooting or was a body found in the woods?"

Gunner looked straight at him and nodded, then turned to Katina and said, "She was found in the park, a single bullet to her head." He glanced back at the laptop and said, "Her body was found March 19."

At her shocked cry of horror, Merk shifted in his chair so he could wrap an arm around Katina and hold her close. "Okay, take it easy. We don't know if it's connected. We obviously have to assume there *could* be a connection, but that doesn't mean that'll happen to you."

"Or to Anna," she said in a shaky voice. "Oh, my God, what have I done?"

In a firm voice, Merk said, "You haven't done anything. It's these assholes who did this."

She turned her glassy gaze to him and said, "But they killed her. Are they planning to do that to me?"

Merk wondered about the best way to answer and then decided there was no gain in making light of it. She needed to be aware. He nodded. "Chances are very good that's exactly what they plan for you. Eventually. They would get that information from you one way or the other."

"But they would only have gotten the key," she whispered. "The rest would have gone to the grave with me." At his surprised look she explained, "If I'm under stress or any duress, my memory doesn't work. I can't recall anything. I have to be calm and feel safe, otherwise ..." She shrugged.

"So not an easy skill to have then," he said.

"And very unreliable. I was getting much better at using it for ... something unrelated," she added cryptically. "But then I got derailed and went home instead."

He turned to look at her, studied her face for a long moment, and then a grin broke out. "You were card-reading in Vegas, weren't you?" he accused. "That's what you meant about Anna being the only one who knew what you were doing there."

Her face fell. She cried out softly, "It occurred to me, when I could memorize all the cards and win a little money, how that might be a way to pay off my student loans, but I wasn't there long enough to even make good on the practice." She sniffled and glared at him, then wiped her eyes in a childish motion that made him smile.

"Card-counting is illegal anyway, so consider me your savior back then too."

She snorted, then turned to Gunner. "If you have anybody you know who could help keep Anna safe, I'd really appreciate it."

He nodded. "I might. Flynn would fit the bill."

Ice gasped in surprise, and then she giggled. "He would at that."

Levi asked, "Is he doing jobs for you? I was hoping to convince him to come work for me. This job could be a good test."

Gunner shook his head. "I'm not taking on jobs. But I know him through Logan. And I know he needs something constructive to do."

"The only thing is, he's a bit of a wild card. That's why he's no longer in the navy," Ice said. "He went rogue on one of his missions, and they decided they couldn't deal with that anymore."

Gunner nodded. "He did, indeed, but for all the right reasons. Some children were stuck in another camp, and his unit had orders to leave them there. Flynn wouldn't listen. He went back and saved them. In the process he lost his career."

"And he's always been a sucker for animals too, hasn't he?" Levi asked. He turned to Ice and said, "He actually was helping out at Dani's Center for a while in the vet clinic."

"Well, then he's got the animal part covered," Ice said. "But he's a bit of a jokester and a ham." Ice turned to study Katina. "What's Anna like? Can she handle somebody with an over-the-top personality?"

"Anna's a bit like that herself. She's quite a firecracker." Katina grinned.

"Seems they'd be perfect together." Ice snorted.

"Hey, we're not in Mason's unit here. No matchmaking allowed," Levi growled at Ice. She smirked in response. His growl deepened as he added, "Like we need that shit."

Merk caught Katina's glance of confusion and told her, "I'll explain later."

To Ice, Merk said, "Nice that you two found each other and got all your shit dealt with. Even nicer that Stone found somebody and had surrendered to all that pain to move on. But don't go matchmaking all the men you know."

Ice just gave him a flat stare, but, in one of those tiny perceptible nods, she managed to include Katina with it. And his glare deepened. But, on the inside, something sparked. And for the first time he realized what their relationship must look like to the others—the way they got along, the way they joked about their past history, and the way he constantly comforted her, and the way she had turned to him. A case could be made for the whole white-knight-in-shining-armor thing but wasn't a basis for a lasting relationship.

Unless he looked at Stone's love life, which began just as suddenly and in a similar fashion.

He shook his head at Ice. "Don't even think it."

She gave him an innocent smile and said, "Don't know what you're talking about."

Levi turned to glance at Merk and said, "No point thinking about it. It's already a fact. Up to you to figure it out." He stood up, outstretched his hand to Ice.

As she stood, she said to Gunner, "If you could contact Flynn, that would be great."

"We're looking to hire another four men, and he was under consideration," Levi said.

"Well, I can't be an active member of your team, which makes me sad," Gunner said. "But, if you need anything, just let me know."

Levi studied him.

Merk knew this was the conversation opener Levi and Ice had been looking for. Merk stood, helped Katina to her feet, and said, "We're going for a walk in the garden. The fresh air will be good for Katina."

He knew they'd take the reasoning the other way around, and they were right. He wanted a few minutes alone with Katina, but, by rights, Katina could use a little bit of space. He led her through the double French doors out to the beautiful garden in the back.

As they stepped through the doors, she said, "Are you taking me away or giving them space?"

He'd always known she was perceptive. Just hadn't realized how perceptive.

Chapter 11

"HOW DO I pay for that security detail?" Katina said as soon as they were out in the bright sunshine.

She turned her face to let the sun's rays bounce off her skin. It was so hard to reconcile the bright sunshine of the outside world and those heavy scary topics going on inside that room. She knew they were one and the same, two sides of the exact same existence, but she'd much rather live in the sunshine.

"Anna doesn't have much money, and neither do I."

"You let us worry about that," Merk said quietly. "Especially if this is the trial run for Flynn. Something we would do anyway. The job's small enough that we can see how he handles it."

She nodded. "So would you take it on as pro bono?"

Merk shrugged. "Sometimes it's what we have to do. Some of our clients can pay, and some can't. It's a matter of balance."

She turned to stare at him. She'd been instantly attracted to him, both times. She looped her arm through his and said, "Let's walk for a bit. It'd be nice to forget all this is happening."

"You've been living with the stress for days, weeks," he said. "That makes it tough on anybody."

"I have but hadn't really realized the repercussions." She

stared off at the roses—a good dozen bushes, all in full bloom. They were beautiful. She reached out to stroke the soft petals. "I feel terrible about Eloise."

"What was she like?"

She turned to look at him. "Nosy. She was one of those people who forever asked questions, like, where you lived. How come you're not married? Did you ever get close to being married?"

She turned her gaze to the daisies and continued, "Initially it was really irritating. But then I realized she was just a gregarious person. She liked to know what everybody else was doing and thinking at any given time. Sometimes I rebuffed her. Sometimes I told her." She shrugged. "I never did tell her about the marriage." She walked over to a bed of beautiful blue flowers and said, "I don't see columbines very much."

She squatted beside the garden and pointed at the different types in front of her. "That's this bed here." She studied them for a long moment, struck by a thought. "They are one of the most delicate-looking flowers. Yet it's amazing how well they survive in harsh conditions. They also reproduce rather easily, considering their fragility."

She straightened and wandered a little bit more. He always stayed a couple steps behind her. Finally, when she got up the courage, she turned and asked, "Do you really think I'm in danger?"

He didn't hold back; he couldn't. "Yes. I do."

She gazed down at her fingers clasped together. "Can I stay with you at the compound, or should I be making arrangements to go somewhere else? Not necessarily my uncle's but someone a long way away?"

"The compound isn't the best idea, but it's better than

leaving the country." His face twisted into a wry smile.

At that, her face scrunched up. "Why?"

"Because it's quite likely to trigger an alert that you're traveling on your passport into Canada." He added cheerfully, "Relax. Levi will be working on a solution. It won't be Canada though."

Sure enough, when they went back inside, the men were all sitting together, making plans. Merk stood in the doorway. "When do we leave?"

Without looking up, Levi said, "This afternoon."

Stepping beside him, Katina asked, "Where are we going?" She slipped her hand into Merk's, loving it when his fingers closed securely around hers.

Levi turned suddenly and looked at her. "If you really want to know, I'll tell you. But it's better if you don't know right now."

"Am I leaving the country?"

He shook his head. "No, we have lots of places around the country we can send people to."

She turned her questioning look at Merk.

He grinned. "Safe houses. We own or have access to a good half dozen of them."

Her mouth was slightly open as she considered this. "Wow. It never occurred to me that was possible." Who knew such a thing existed outside law enforcement?

Just then a manservant walked into the room and said, "Lunch will be in ten minutes."

Gunner waved a hand in his direction and said, "Thanks, Bruno."

Katina watched the massive male walk back out. "Are you guys all on steroids or something? How the hell does everybody get to be that size?"

"When you're used to working with only military per-sonnel," Merk said, "it's natural to have friends and people you trust and to keep them around afterward. In Gunner's case, he's employed many of his ex-military associates."

"Already trained, understand loyalty, and know how to keep quiet, right?"

Merk looked down at her and grinned. "Exactly."

Five minutes later they walked into a large dining room.

Merk led her to the table, set and ready for them. Very quickly the rest of the room filled up—with a lot more people than she had seen so far. A cold luncheon of sand-wiches, salads, sausage rolls, and pies was spread before them. In fact it all looked delicious. And she was starving.

She watched as Merk carefully served himself a couple sandwiches and rolls, then nudged him with her elbow and said, "Please."

With a smile he added a couple things to her plate. She looked at him with a sorrowful gaze. He laughed and added another one.

At the far end of the table Gunner spoke up. "There's lots of food, Katina. You won't starve here."

"Good thing," she said with a big grin, "because I'm hungry. I'd probably outeat Merk in a heartbeat."

"She probably could," Merk said with a laugh.

That set the tone for the lunch. Lighthearted conversa-tion, good food. All followed by a tray of desserts with some wonderful roasted coffee. She didn't know what kind it was, but it was rich and thick. She sat back and smiled. "You do know how to live, Gunner."

"My dear," he said in a very serious voice, "after a lot of years thinking I was likely to die ..." Then to another he said, "I learned a very hard lesson. And it's all about living every day as if it's your last. And it makes for a very good living." He lifted his glass of wine and held it up and said, "Cheers."

She lifted her coffee cup. "I haven't learned that lesson yet. It seems like all I've done for weeks is run."

"There will be an end to this," he promised.

Less than an hour later they were in the truck, heading back toward the compound. Levi and Ice stayed behind to work on a few things. Katina figured it would also give them a chance to get ahead slightly so they could see if anybody was following them. It just felt odd to know she was part of a convoy at all times. But it also felt good. She felt secure.

And now, for the first time in a long time, she had people who she could trust to help her. What a heady feeling.

When they pulled into the compound, she no longer had the same sense of shock. Until she realized her car was gone. She gasped. "Where's my car?"

"Alfred moved it into one of the garages while we were gone, so it's out of sight."

"Oh." She slumped back down again. "I wouldn't have thought of that."

"Yes, you would've. Just not right off the bat. And you don't have to think about it now. This is what we do. Trust us to do it."

She nodded. As he parked and turned off the engine, he turned to her and said, "Now go and pack. You can have two bags maximum—one big and one small. Pack for cold evenings but hot days."

She frowned. "Cold evenings or just sweater-cool evenings?" She shook her head. "I don't think I have anything for cold evenings."

"Sweaters will be fine."

She opened the door and eased out. Together they walked into the compound. Sienna, Stone, Lissa, and Alfred waited for them. Lissa handed Merk a notepad and an envelope. "Contacts, keys, company card."

Stone said, "You're switching to a rental in Houston." He handed over the information.

Merk nodded, accepted both and said, "We'll pack and leave in thirty minutes."

Alfred stepped forward with a large basket in his hand. He handed it to Merk. "Traveling food. If you need more, you'll have to stop and pick up something along the way."

Merk stared at the size of the basket and chuckled. "I know she likes to eat, guys, but …"

"This hopefully will last you for your first day," Alfred said. "After that, you'll have to shop."

Sienna smiled at Katina. "How do you feel about becoming a brunette?"

Katina's eyebrows shot up, but she understood immediately. "I'd rather be a redhead, but brunette is just fine."

The two women headed to her room. Sienna managed to dye and rinse Katina's hair, then blow-dried it enough that Katina could braid it and not have a sopping-wet braid dripping down her back. She quickly changed into traveling clothes with a sweater and sneakers. She kept her jeans on and had a T-shirt under the sweater. Then she packed.

With a bag in each hand, she cast a final glance around the room and turned to stare at Sienna. "I guess I'm ready."

Sienna led her out into the hallway, saying, "You'll be just fine. Merk will look after you."

"I know. He always did before."

"I think it's great that you two were married. Obviously something is still there."

Katina shook her head. "I don't know. That one night was great, but we divorced the next morning. ... That was brutal."

The two burst into laughter as they met the group in the hallway. Merk stood there with his bags ready to go.

He looked at her, nodding. "Nice hair." He grinned and asked, "Shall we?"

"Thanks." She took a deep breath and said, "Yes, absolutely."

INTERESTING. HE'D WONDERED if she would renege at the very last moment, but apparently she'd decided to put her trust in them and was prepared to follow his lead. Good. It would make things a whole lot easier if he didn't have to fight her. Because he had every intention of protecting her, whether she wanted him to or not.

With everything loaded and both of them buckled up, he honked the horn lightly. He knew Levi and the unit were tracking the vehicle. They'd follow Merk straight through.

He and Katina were heading to New Mexico, not too long a drive but long enough. By the time they hit the main highway, he told her they had several hours of driving, so she settled in the front seat.

"Did Gunner ever connect Flynn to Anna?"

"I understand Gunner was talking to him. I don't know what the end result was. As soon as they have something settled, they'll let us know."

"Sure. And in the meantime, what happens to Anna?" She turned to study Merk and added, "Maybe we should stay with her until they get somebody."

He shook his head. "No. We're taking you out of here.

Flynn will help Anna."

He didn't bother to look her way. The car doors were locked, and they escaped the city, traveling full speed ahead. No way in hell were they going back to babysit. Somebody else could do that job. He trusted Levi to make that happen.

"Did you ever contact your uncle?" he asked. He hated to bring up the subject, but it was possible somebody would go after him.

"He travels a lot normally, so I don't know if he'd be home right now. Plus I was still afraid to lead trouble to him." She sighed. "A whole lot of negative possibilities are crowding my mind, worrying how something is wrong."

"Don't borrow any trouble right now. We have enough to go around."

Her laugh was bitter. "You think? If anybody else I know dies …"

"Don't think about it," he said firmly.

He drove steadily, stopping in Washington, Texas, for a gas break once. When they got back in the truck, she looked at the basket, then at him, and asked, "Shall I check out what Alfred packed for us?"

He waved his hand. "Absolutely. I'm feeling hungry myself."

She dove into the basket and pulled out large sandwiches beautifully wrapped up, a thermos with maybe two servings of something, and what looked like a selection of savory pies and handmade pastries. Her coos of delight made him smile.

"Alfred is one hell of a cook." She quickly unpacked a sandwich and handed him a half.

As he studied the creation in his hand—a great big thick black multigrain bread full of vegetables and meat and cheese—Merk nodded. "That he is."

They munched down their halves in no time. She was kept busy opening a second sandwich and then a third. He figured she had to be full, because she'd stopped opening sandwiches, only to find her examining the small pies. She handed him one and then took the second one for herself. Looked to be miniature quiches. He had his done in about three bites, but she curled up in the corner and moaned as she slowly ate hers.

He grinned. She was very sensuous in all she did. Just another example of what intrigued him. With the first wave of hunger taken care of, she could sit back, relax, and enjoy her quiche.

He really liked that about her. A time to be high-pressured and a time to be eased back. She seemed to follow her instincts in a natural rhythm that allowed for that type of on/off temperament.

That was a good thing. If she could relax right now, he hoped that also meant she could be ready to run at a moment's notice. Lord knew he might need her too.

As far as he could tell, they hadn't been followed.

But that didn't mean someone wasn't searching for them.

He had to get to the new location as fast as possible and hide out there. Maybe for weeks. Was she aware of that?

On the other hand, he was okay with it and was looking forward to spending time alone with her. All the guys would forgive him for thinking it was an opportunity too good to pass up. He knew they'd been dynamite in bed together. Now all he could think about was if she had changed and matured so much in bed and would he like that much better too? After all, he loved this older model of her already ...

He gave a quiet snort. He was a fool. Because even if she

wasn't exactly the same as she was before, she'd be damn hot now too. And one thing hadn't changed—he wanted her any way he could have her.

Chapter 12

THEY PULLED INTO one of the outlying subdivisions of Albuquerque. She loved the change of scenery. It was really stunning. Not to mention the reddish color of the hills. When he drove up to a small adobe house tucked into the hillside, she smiled. "Is this where we're staying? It's adorable."

He nodded. "Yes, this is one of ours."

"And you guys just come and holiday here? Perfect."

He shook his head. "We travel the world over," he said. "There are other places to holiday."

She sighed. "I'm a simple girl. This suits my heart just fine." She opened her door of the truck and slid out.

"Wait," he ordered sharply. "Let me check that it's all good."

At that, she froze. His words reminded her how she wasn't on holiday in any way, shape, or form. She stood at the truck and waited.

He walked toward the front entryway and quickly unlocked the door and stepped inside. She didn't know what to think. She understood why they were here, but, for just a moment, it had been nice to think it was an entirely different reason. When he stepped back out again and gave her a big smile, she knew they were good.

Reaching in the truck, she pulled out the basket Alfred

had sent with them. It was still heavily laden, but she knew it wouldn't last more than a day or so. She carried that up and stepped into the front of the house as he walked back to the truck to grab her bags. An Aztec theme decorated the inside, nice and simple with interesting floors, and what looked like plaster walls with stone and brick mixed in. A bit of old mixed with a bit of new.

She loved it.

All of it.

She set down the basket and explored the place. Three bedrooms were upstairs, one with a bath, and the other two shared a bath between them. As she looked out the windows at the small community nestled in the foothills, she just smiled to herself. She hadn't had a chance to go many places in her life, and she'd never been to New Mexico. It was perfect. No, it was better than perfect. It might not be a holiday, but she was damned if she wouldn't enjoy this.

Still laughing greedily like a fool, she ran downstairs and unpacked the basket. As she watched, smiling, Merk carried the bags upstairs. Good. He could take one of the bedrooms with the shared bath. She wanted the suite. But that was hardly fair.

When she had emptied the basket and had put away the food in the fridge and cupboards, she noticed the coffeepot and a bag of ground coffee. Even better. She immediately set up for coffee and realized she had no idea how much to put in. She made a good guess. She could always adjust the amount for the next pot.

When it was done, she still had no sign of Merk; she figured he'd gotten lost on his computer or talking to his unit back at the compound. She poured two cups and went in search of him. Sure enough, she found a room in the back on the main floor established as an office.

He had his laptop and gear ready to go. With his headset on, he talked to Levi. "Okay, that's good to know. I'll tell her Flynn is already at the shelter." He listened a bit, then a grin flashed on his face.

She placed his coffee on the desk.

"Let the sparks fly with those two," he said. "I'll give you an update once we settle in and head into town to do some shopping. I'll check in with Freddy when I'm there."

He hung up soon afterward and said, "Thanks for the coffee."

"What was that about Anna?" Katina asked.

"Flynn agreed to give her personal security." He paused for a second. "I guess the meeting wasn't too friendly. She didn't take very kindly to his presence."

Katina winced. "I should've warned her. If he walked in with any arrogance, she'd have chopped him to pieces."

Merk laughed. "He definitely walked in with that. He's a character and a half. But he's a good man. He's an even better soldier."

"Okay then, the rest doesn't really matter. As long as she stays safe. She might hate me when this is over, but that means she's alive, and I'm good with that."

"Levi wants you to make contact with your uncle," Merk said. "Just to be sure he's safe."

She took out her phone right then and found her uncle's number. Once again it rang and rang. "No answer," she said to Merk. "And no voice mail."

"Okay, what's his name? I'll send the details to Ice and Levi—see if they can track his passport."

She quickly gave him the name, address, and phone number. "Maybe somebody could physically check to see he's all right?" she asked quietly. "He lives out in the country, so it needs to be the RCMP that stops by."

He nodded. "No idea if Levi knows someone up there or not."

"I am pretty damn sure Levi knows somebody everywhere," she said with a snort. "That man has connections."

"He has. Gunner might help too."

"And didn't you say you had somebody in England?" she asked, having only a hazy idea of how that all worked.

"That would be Charles in England, and he might very well have some idea of how to track your uncle down too." Merk frowned and continued to type.

She didn't know if he was emailing or if he was in a secure chat room. All the stuff they did was way over her head.

"Ice has news. Several of the board members of Bristol and Partners, Ltd. were in a private plane crash. The authorities assume there were no survivors." He raised that piercing gaze to study her. "Did you ever meet any of them?"

She sank slowly into a chair and stared at him in shock. "I don't know. We had CEOs where I worked, but I don't know that any were the head of Bristol." She shook her head. "I didn't really have anything to do with any of the board members. I'm not sure I even know their names."

He nodded. "And this may have nothing to do with what information you've gathered."

"On the other hand, how could it not?" she asked. "Just think about it. I find all this information, and people connected to that same company are dropping dead now." She shook her head, staring out the window closest to him, studying the rock formations, not really seeing them. "I wonder what kind of shakedowns are happening in the company? Were those people, the directors, the ones responsible for the information I found?"

"Stop," he said sharply. "This is not your fault."

She turned her gaze back to him, but her lower lip trembled. "You sure? But, if I had just left it alone … It's just money. So what if they were stealing money, evading taxes? Do I really care?" She shook her head. "Not when compared to the loss of life."

"And you don't get to ask that question," he said quietly. "Because if they had done this already, you have no idea what else they've done—like Eloise. And, for all you know, some of this money is being laundered from drug deals or sex-trafficking rings. At this point, somebody has to take a stand and shut it down. You've done that. Don't second-guess yourself now. This is too damn important."

She stared at her hands. "I know that. Really I do. It's just hard to see the cause-and-effect of one's own actions."

"Standing on the side of right, you'll never have to question that again. Because, even if you don't know the outcome, you have to believe what you are doing is the right thing." He took off his headset and stood. "Let's go for a walk. It's a beautiful little town. Nobody knows who we are, and we can play tourist."

She finished her coffee in several gulps and said, "That would be lovely." She put the two cups back into the kitchen and turned off the pot.

At the front door, she stopped and looked around. Hard to imagine they could possibly not be safe here with the idyllic sleepiness to the area.

Merk stepped up beside her, locked the door, then held out his hand. Without hesitation she placed hers in his. And together they walked into town.

HE HAD WORRIED about telling her of the plane crash. Knew it would be hard to hear that other people were suffering or had been killed because of her actions. But she couldn't look at it that way. Because that was not how reality was. These people had set themselves on this path a long time ago. He didn't know if the plane crash was connected. But, like her, he had to assume it was. The coincidence was a little too damning. Like Eloise's execution.

Merk led Katina down a series of narrow pathways. He'd spent a week here a year ago and had really enjoyed it. This was a lovely place to hide out for a few days.

He had several other locations, and, if this one got compromised, they would pick up and move again. But, for right now, he planned to take her for dinner at a great little restaurant downtown.

It was late afternoon. If they were lucky he could get to the repair shop and find Freddy. Afterward they had a chance to explore a little, then they could sit down, eat, and rest. Everything could be done here on foot; no need to drive around. That would help, because he was driving a big-ass truck, and, though trucks were common here, it would be obvious they were strangers in town.

What a beautiful time of year with the gardens and the trees. Not that there was much in the way of trees, but the little bit there were, they were bright and cheerful. The afternoon brought a low-level heat. He'd told her to bring cold-weather clothes, but, at the time, he figured they were heading to the Colorado Mountains. At night it would still be cold here. He hoped she also brought T-shirts and shorts.

Once they'd walked through town, and she had a chance to admire the quaintness and the simplicity of the place, he led her to a TV repair shop at the far end. He was glad

Freddy didn't have to rely on this business for his income. Not many people repaired TVs anymore. They were a disposable commodity nowadays.

He did repair other electronics, but, as far as Merk was concerned, damn near all broken electronics—other than computers you could rebuild yourself—fell into the same category: garbage. He pushed open the door and let her enter ahead of him.

Once inside the dingy room, he turned to study the walls of dusty electronics. Not a great disguise for what really went on in the back of the store but seemed to work for Freddy. At the front counter Merk hit the bell. And waited. Finally he heard shuffling in the back. And that was actually reassuring as it meant Freddy was still here.

As he waited, the old man stepped through the long lines of beadwork, letting them jangle as they dropped back into place. Merk watched Katina's face as she studied the beadwork and smiled. Merk turned toward Freddy and said, "Long time no see, Fred."

Freddy's face lit up beautifully. They reached across the counter and shook hands. Merk placed an arm around Katina's shoulders and tucked her up against him. "And this is Katina, my girlfriend," he said with a big smile. He found it interesting that he saw no sign of surprise from Katina. But, then again, they had to play roles of some kind. This one just made sense. The only question was, how committed a relationship was he going to try to pull off? He figured "girlfriend" had to be the easiest on her.

"What the hell are you doing in town?" Freddy asked with a big grin that showed missing front teeth.

Freddy had been a bruiser in his day, a boxer in a ring where he lost teeth, busted some bones, and had taken more than a few blows to his head. But, unlike a lot of prizefighters, he was still going strong in his late 60s.

Merk knew one of these days he'd come into town and find that nobody would answer the ring of the bell. "We're just here for a week's holiday," Merk said. "Getting away from the stresses of life. Needed to relax a bit."

Freddy nodded sagely. "Stress will kill you," he warned. "Been telling you to move to the country and farm or something."

Merk gave a booming laugh. "I don't think farming and I would get along. I might handle the machinery just fine, but dealing with the animals and planting the acres? No way."

Freddy cackled. "No, no, you don't look much like a gardener to me." He studied Katina and gave her a toothless grin. "How did you ever get hung up with this guy? You sure somebody better wasn't around?"

She gave him a beautiful smile and said, "No, I never had any doubt. Merk is for me."

Merk clenched his fingers around her shoulder a little tighter than he expected. But her words pierced his protective shield. She was either a damn good actress or she meant what she had said. He desperately wanted to ask her which.

They exchanged a few more banalities, then Merk said, "Anything new happening around here?"

"What kind of time frame you talking?" Freddy asked, immediately getting down to business. "Last twenty-four hours?"

"We just arrived, so it'd be nice to know if anything came in ahead of us."

Freddy shook his head. "Nothing I've heard. No strangers, no new vehicles, but, you know, it's early days yet.

Be warned."

Merk nodded. "Give us a heads-up if you hear anything."

"Or see something?" Freddy asked. His piercing-blue gaze narrowed. "I've got some new equipment if you want to take a look."

Merk wanted to take a look badly. He nodded his head casually. "Sure, love to."

Freddy led them to the back of the store, and Merk smiled at Katina's gasp of surprise. As the front had been a dusty, dodgy old store where nobody seemed to give a damn; the back room was entirely the opposite—everything gleamed, shiny and bright—and full of top-of-the-line electronics.

Merk walked over to one of the huge monitors set up on a system off to the left and said, "Satellite? How did you get the connection?"

"*Connection* is the truth behind that statement. But I never give out my sources." He cackled and sat down in his chair. With a couple clicks they had an overview of the entire town. He shifted the cameras to the house they were staying in. "Now would you look at that?" Freddy asked.

"Looks damn fine. You've certainly had some upgrades since I was here last."

"Yep. I work for my friends, all over the world. Any excuse for new equipment is a reason to buy new toys."

Merk laughed. "That is the truth." He leaned in to study the town, realizing they could see people walking along the streets. He didn't recognize anybody.

Freddy said, "You're still using the same phone?"

"I'll give you a new number." He quickly rattled off the one for the phone he kept in his pocket. "If there's any emergency, use that number and call me immediately."

"Will do. Who am I charging?"

"Call Ice. I think it's still all the same accounts, but who knows? That's her stuff."

"You got it. By the way, this new little restaurant is in town down that way. French bistro," he said with a twist of his lips as he accented the last word. "I don't know the name. Most of the dishes have a fancy name no one can pronounce, but the food tastes damn good."

On that note, Merk turned Katina around and led her toward the front door. At the last moment he turned and said, "Anything interesting in the last year around here?"

Freddy shook his head. "Nope. The place is dead. And that's the way I like it. I'll be joining it soon." And he cackled with laughter.

"Anything in other parts of the world that might interest me?"

Freddy narrowed his gaze and studied him, then said, "Maybe. Let me think about that."

Merk nodded. Freddy was always a good source of information and normally the unusual stuff. "I have another address of interest. Wouldn't mind if you keep an eye out for it."

Freddy nodded. "Extra charges though."

Merk nodded. "That's not my problem. Ice won't have a problem either. Just call her." He rattled off the name of the shelter and the address. "The owner running the place is a potential connection to a murder case with long tentacles."

Freddy frowned. "I got no truck with that. Nobody should be touching women in this day and age. The fact that she's running an animal shelter, yeah, that's just low. I'll do this one for free." He snickered. "I presume you have somebody there on guard?"

That's when Merk remembered that Freddy knew Flynn and had to laugh. "You'll like this. Flynn's there."

Freddy's jaw dropped open. "Ha! Now that's perfect. What the hell did you do to get him to agree to that?"

Merk shook his head. "I didn't have anything to do with it. Levi did."

"Where the hell's Logan? I figured he'd be here with you."

Merk smirked. "Logan is in California, protecting some entertainer. A singer, I believe."

Freddy's jaw dropped for the second time. "Really? That's just too funny. Who'd have thought Logan would've fallen so bad that he'd be bodyguarding?"

Merk said, "There's no way I could do it, but somebody has to, and Logan was picked." Merk shook his head. "I think she might've known him before. So ..." He shrugged. "Logan got the short straw on that one."

Freddy chuckled. "I'm glad you stopped by. Haven't had this much fun for a long time. Just thinking about those two guys will keep me in laughter for years."

With a wave, Merk led Katina from the store. Walking down the sidewalk of the main street toward the restaurant, she said, "What the hell was that all about?"

He chuckled. "Just somebody else who the world doesn't have a clue about, but one who keeps an eye on the world. We've used Freddy for years. Levi has known him for decades. With any luck he'll still be around another couple decades because, when it comes to keeping an eye in the sky, he's dynamite."

"So can he really keep watch on our place and on Anna?"

"And on the compound," he said with a smile. "And, if

we can establish that your uncle is home, then Freddy'll keep an eye on him too."

"I had no idea such things were possible," she explained. "And, if I had known, I would've assumed it was done by a government agency, like a supersecret spy organization."

"In a way that's what we are. Don't forget, we were all top military in the past. We just transferred those skills to the private civilian arena. Getting the equipment and setting up the electronics, now that was a bit of a challenge. But we're slowly getting there." He tucked her arm into his and said, "People like Freddy give us the opportunity to do what we do. And that's to help people like you. Now a small place just around the corner is where I want to take you for dinner."

"Did you say dinner?" she said with a drawl of humor. "I was tempted to snack when I unpacked Alfred's basket but held off. I'm starved."

"I have no idea where you put it." Still, he liked to see a woman eat. He'd had enough of the kind who worried about eating a small salad. He understood the need to maintain whatever image the women were working on, but to be with somebody who didn't give a damn was a nice breath of fresh air—and still looked great.

He kept an eye out for anyone following them or appearing to watch them a little too closely. He didn't expect to find anything wrong this fast, but it was always possible. Particularly after meeting up with Freddy. If Merk was on anyone's radar, just going into Freddy's shop would trigger interest.

The restaurant was up ahead and around the corner. He pointed at the various stores. "This town is lost in time. They make fudge by hand, and a couple little coffee places still do the old-fashioned moka pot coffees, if you want an espresso the classic Italian way."

"Yes, to all of it," she said with a smile. "Hopefully we can try something different every day."

"That's exactly what I intend. No reason we can't enjoy our time here."

"Am I still to pretend I'm your girlfriend?" she teased. "Even when we're not with Freddy?"

"It's even more important to do so when we're not with Freddy. Freddy's the one who understands." He turned to look at her. "Will that be hard?"

"No," she said with a smile. "Honestly I have been clinging to your side for days now. Nothing's really different, except for unexpected memories I had never thought to revisit."

At the entranceway to the restaurant, he stopped and checked it out. "A little early for dinner. Do you want to go in and eat or keep walking?"

"Let's go in and eat. A walk afterward would be nice, and then we can head home. That should help me digest whatever it is I happen to be inhaling for dinner," she said with a smile.

He held the door open and ushered her in. After a final glance around he followed her. This was one of the cozy cafés, but the food had always been good. Assuming his memory served him well.

Soon they were settled at a small table by a big window. They could look down the street and see if anybody walked by. Few people were out as most folks had gone home for the day.

When the menu was placed in front of her, she leaned forward and said, "You do realize we didn't stop at the bank, and I don't have very much in the way of money."

He reached across and covered her hand with his. "And you do realize that you're not allowed to touch your cards at any point in time? Because anyone searching for you can trace when your cards are used. So this week you are to forget about money. We will cover the cost of everything. And, yes, that means you still get to eat."

Merk motioned toward the menu. "Order what you want."

Chapter 13

WALKING BACK AFTER dinner was a good idea, as her stomach needed to settle. The food was excellent but rich. She was afraid it would upset her system.

By the time they walked into the house, she felt fatigue pulling at her. Now that they were safe and a long way from the danger, the waves of tension and stress rolled off her back, taking all her energy with them. She yawned. "Sorry. That came out of nowhere."

She snuggled in close when Merk wrapped an arm around her shoulder. "You've been running on empty for a long time. A good night's sleep will help."

"Do we have anything set to do on any of the days we're here?" she asked. "Or can we just relax, go for walks, and sit and talk?"

"I have work to do on the laptop but, other than that, no. This is downtime."

"Oh, good." She tossed him a sideways glance and grinned. "Don't wake me up before ten tomorrow morning."

He looked at her, his eyebrows raised. "Are you serious? Ten o'clock? That's like noon." But he grinned wildly.

"So not noon. Inasmuch as I want to say ten o'clock, chances are I'll be awake at eight anyway."

"Well, I'll be up at six, so it doesn't matter. You can sleep as late as you need to."

She put a pot of water on the stove and searched the cupboards for tea. She found a few suspicious tea bags but wasn't sure she wanted to try them. However, Alfred had put some fresh lemons in the basket. She sliced one and made herself hot lemon water.

Merk watched her and said, "What were you looking for?"

"Tea, but it doesn't matter."

"We'll go shopping tomorrow." He searched the cupboards to see what was here, as if mentally doing a list in his head. He stopped at the fridge, saw the amount of food Alfred had packed which was still uneaten. "Actually, if we go out for one meal a day, we'll probably have food for the rest of the week," he exclaimed. "Alfred must think we eat a ton."

"Well, it seemed we ate almost one-third on the way up." She laughed. "He isn't far from wrong."

She took her lemon drink into the living room and sat down on the big couch. Merk sprawled out on the opposite couch. It wasn't very late, and, though she was tired, she wasn't quite tired enough to go to sleep. She pulled one of the pillows close to her and stretched out. "What did you do right after you left Vegas?" she asked curiously.

"Reported for duty." He turned to look at her. "I'd been serious. I was headed for my training immediately afterward."

She nodded. "I didn't think you'd lied."

"In Vegas, I think we have to expect there'd be lies."

That got a laugh out of her. "Since I was in college at the time, I just returned to campus with Anna and the other girls down there with us. Because we'd been in a group, my absence wasn't noticed like it would have been if it had been just Anna and me. They saw you and me, of course, so I was bugged decently on the way home, but I never said a word."

"But you did tell Anna about us?"

"I did but not right away." She raked her fingers through her hair, letting the strands of braid fall apart. "And it's a good thing I waited because she was pretty shocked and horrified as it was. If I had told her about it right away, she'd have screamed all the way home."

Katina smiled as she remembered. "When I called her a firecracker, I meant it. She spouted lots and blasted me for being a fool and a number of different names, but she's a really good person inside. When she calmed down, she wanted to know exactly how to get me clear of you."

"Does she know I'm in your life again?"

"Not in that way."

She realized that, although she'd told Anna that she was with Merk, but not in that way, it meant something different. She quickly added, "Just what you heard on the phone call."

"Ah." He settled back on the couch.

"Did you tell anybody back then?" she asked.

"Only my brother, Terkel. First off, I was headed for training. I didn't know anybody else around, so I had nobody to tell. By the time I met up with old friends, it wasn't something I wanted to bring up," he said drily. "Later I told my brother, but then he had a good idea already."

"Wow, really?"

He quickly explained about Terkel's "intuition" and their Creole grandma with the sight. That brought up several more questions. By the time they ran out of topics, they lay in companionable silence while she drank her hot lemon water. When she finished, she said, "I think I'll try to sleep now." She held up her phone and said, "Thanks for this phone."

"Not an issue. We also put a tracker in that for our purposes, in case you get separated from us so we can locate you," he said. "Just remember you can't do is tell anybody where you are."

"Right, secrecy." She stood up and carried her cup back to the kitchen and rinsed it out. Turning to him again, she said, "I'll shower and get into bed. I can always surf the web on my phone until I fall asleep." She walked to the stairs and called back, "Good night."

At the first landing she heard Merk say, "Good night. Have a good sleep." And caught sight of him heading back to his office.

She should have gone to her room earlier. He obviously had work to do and didn't feel he could do it while she was with him.

At the top of stairs she wondered where he'd put her bags, but, as she glanced into the master bedroom, she realized he'd given her the suite. She smiled in delight. This house wasn't fancy, but it was different. And she really appreciated those differences.

Wandering into the bathroom, she squealed in delight at the really big bathtub. "This is what I'll do first."

She closed the bedroom door and quickly unpacked the few things she'd brought. If she would be here five or six days, she might as well enjoy it.

She bent down to plug the tub and then turned on the water. A selection of bubble bath packets and bath oils were on the side. She chose one, dumped in a liberal amount. She found a guest bathrobe, brought it in the bathroom with her, and quickly stripped down. When she settled herself into the bubble bath, she gave a moan of delight.

How long had it been since she'd just sat back and relaxed and enjoyed the moment? It seemed like forever.

She could hear voices below, but she presumed Merk was on the phone using the Speaker option. They hadn't had any visitors, and she hadn't heard anybody else come in.

She lay in the water until it cooled and then dressed in her nightclothes, which consisted of panties and an oversize T-shirt, and crawled into bed. Within minutes, she turned out the lights and tried to sleep.

But she couldn't. Not that she wasn't tired, because she was, and not that she wasn't relaxed, because she was. She just couldn't shut off her mind. Knowing so much had happened, and, just because she had the chance to shut everything down and rest, it didn't mean it was so easy to do. She got up and grabbed her laptop, turning it on. She couldn't really reply to the emails, other than to tell people she was fine and off on a vacation.

With that done, she brought up a webpage and checked out this area of New Mexico. What were the attractions? They should have picked up a brochure in one of the stores, but she hadn't thought of it at the time. With the lamp on, the pillow bunched up behind her back, she was comfy and cozy in bed.

Light footsteps sounded outside her door. She smiled. She already recognized Merk's approach. At the knock on her door, she said, "Come in."

Merk pushed open the door and stuck his head around the wooden panel. "I thought you'd be asleep by now."

"I can't sleep. I did try, but my head just won't shut down. So I did some web surfing, finding out more about this place and seeing what there was to do."

He frowned at the laptop. "That's the first I've seen you with a laptop."

"Oh." She peered over the top of the screen at him. "Does it matter?"

"Not unless it's being tracked." He slowly approached, his gaze on the machine in her hands.

"I've never taken it to work, and I lived alone, so I don't know how someone would've put in a tracking device."

"How long have you had it?"

"Over a year. This laptop is where I saw the first email asking me, *Where is it?*"

Interest piqued in his gaze. "Do you have those emails?"

She nodded and brought up her email program. She'd actually filed all the emails in specific folders. She brought up the folder and opened it so he could see. She turned the laptop slightly so he could have a better view.

"Do you mind?" he asked with his hands out.

She handed him the laptop. Drawing her knees up to her chest, she waited while he searched through the emails.

"I'll forward these to Levi, if you're okay with that."

She nodded. "I would have done it earlier if I knew you needed them."

"I understand. This comes under the heading of *you don't know what you need to know if you don't ask the right questions.*"

"Exactly." At least he wasn't blaming her for not having shown him earlier. She would have, but it had slipped her mind and obviously had slipped theirs as well. She waited in silence for him to finish whatever he was doing.

"Is there anything else on this laptop that would be of interest?"

She glanced from the laptop to him and frowned. "I

can't imagine that there would be, but feel free to look around."

She only had the one laptop because she assumed she'd need it, but, in truth, she never really did. She played some games on it, wrote a few emails, but she had a work laptop and that's where she spent most of her time. In truth, she'd wondered about just getting a tablet next time.

THEY WENT TO the office where he plugged in a second machine and set up a program to run through her laptop. It did a couple searches, plus a diagnostic. He doubted there'd be any trackers, but he wasn't taking any chances. Somebody had obviously known her personal email address and had sent these anonymous emails to her. They were of interest only for the fact that somebody knew she had something she wasn't supposed to have.

He glanced at her and said, "Go on to bed. This will take a while."

She crossed her arms over her chest and tapped her foot lightly on the floor. "In no known universe are you allowed to give me orders and I am to follow them."

He glanced at her in surprise, then grinned. "I always liked that spunk in you."

She snorted and sat down. "You didn't have long to like anything about me. Let's get real. We had sex. We got married. We had more sex. We got divorced, and we parted. The end."

He laughed. "We certainly didn't need the paperwork to have sex," he said with a leer. "We could have done just fine without that."

"Sad but true. I haven't had a drop of tequila since."

He shook his head. "Neither have I."

The two smiled in understanding at each other. He really loved the fact that they could joke about it like they were. In a casual tone, his gaze on the laptops in front of them, he said, "Did you ever wonder if we should have adjusted, you know, to being married and given it a try?" Because he wasn't looking at her, he hadn't really registered her response until the odd silence came through. He lifted his gaze and studied her.

And then she cracked up.

Slightly affronted he asked, "What? What did I say?"

She giggled. "You thinking that maybe we should have given it a shot." She shook her head as mirth shook her shoulders. "What, another shot of tequila?"

"I wasn't that drunk."

"Yes, you were. And so was I." When she finally sputtered to a stop, her shoulders slightly shaking with the humor still in her, she added, "I never gave it a serious thought. I wondered what the hell I was thinking in the first place, but I never thought about prolonging that madness by staying married to you."

He wondered if he was supposed to be insulted over that. "Was I such a poor catch?"

"I have no idea," she said candidly. "It's not like we knew each other at all. We don't know the first thing about each other."

"But something lured us together," he said honestly. "Not just a physical attraction—but I really liked that too. You were funny. You were honest. Something about you was just"—he shrugged his shoulders—"attractive."

"A man of few words," she said with a smile. "But you're right. We had a good time, then it was over."

He nodded and gazed at the laptops. "Still, a part of me wonders *what if?*" he said.

"It's too late to wonder *what if?*" she said calmly. "You've moved on and probably had a dozen-plus relationships since, and I've moved on and had a couple." She looked at him pointedly. "And, if you're honest with yourself, you know there was no future for us."

"Back then," he admitted. "But I'm not that person anymore." He waved his arms wide open to encompass the house. "Although the work I did and now do are similar," he said, his smile widening, "back then I wasn't thinking permanency either. Through the years, when—or if—I was out on dangerous missions, I had short-term relationships because I never knew if, one time, I wasn't coming back."

Instantly her humor died. "Were your missions that dangerous?"

He eyed her slowly and then nodded. "Yes. They were generally. We did what nobody else could do. When the final mission blew up in our faces, in a way, I figured it was something I had expected all along to happen, which had finally happened, and we deserved it. We had luck with us for so long, but we knew, at one point, our luck would run out."

"Did you have good luck charms or something to keep you safe?" she asked, half-joking.

"I had something better actually. My brother."

At that, she leaned forward, interest in her eyes. "What do you mean? Was he on the mission with you?"

"No. Remember my brother has my grandmother's gift of sight? He often warned us ahead of time if things would go sideways."

"Did he warn you on this one?"

He stared at her for a long moment and then nodded. "He said he could see something was really bad about the whole deal. But we couldn't take the chance of those people getting away. Terkel told us not to go, but we all made the decision to go anyway."

"Even after he told you not to? I bet he didn't think much of that."

"No, he hasn't warned us too much since," Merk said. "He said something about us not wasting his time. If he gives us intel, we should make good use of it."

"I bet he tells you if it's important though." She sat back and nodded. "Families are like that."

"How do you know? You don't have much family."

"I used to. My parents divorced a long time ago. I was bounced from one home to the other. They both had new families, and I was this third wheel, hanging on from a previous life that neither wanted to acknowledge." She stared out the window and said, "I left as soon as I could. Not for me." She waved her hand. "Now they have completely different partners."

"So you didn't go to them when you had trouble."

Her gaze zinged in his direction again. She said with absolute finality, "No."

He nodded. "My brother and I are quite close. We're twins actually. But he got the gift of sight, and I didn't." It never really bothered him until that mission blew up in his face. If only he'd listened, he would have stopped the entire team from going. But it seemed like he was bullheaded, filled with drive and ambition. And stupidity.

"Anybody else besides your brother has that insight?"

Merk shook his head. "No, and my grandmother passed away a couple years back."

"Did she know? Did she see what was coming for herself?"

"I don't know if she did," he admitted. "She died when I was on a mission. But what I do know is Terkel knew. He warned me that she would go while I was out of the country, and the following week she passed away."

She smiled knowingly at him.

"What are you smiling at?"

"Because I know you went to see her before it happened, didn't you?"

He leaned back in his chair and glared at her. "You don't know that."

"Yes, I do. You're just that kind of guy."

Chapter 14

KATINA WOKE THE next morning with a smile on her face. She'd slept like a dream. She'd left the office last night soon after their conversation and went up to bed. Her mood was lighthearted and fun. She was afraid she was falling for him all over again. No, she knew she was. He was right. They had come together for a reason in the first place, and that attraction was hard to let go of. Even now that same feeling still remained over a decade later. It was just amazing.

Now that he brought it up, she had to wonder *what if?*

As she lay in bed, the morning sun shining on her face, she realized one *what if* was that she could have had a family and a loving life. Living the dream.

Alternatively that might have changed something in his world, and he would not be doing the work he was doing, or he could have been killed on a mission because something about her had distracted him.

In reality, she understood that things happened for a reason. But that gave her leeway to think that maybe they had come together for a second chance for another reason. That she was sleeping alone here was also unique because Merk had been a hotheaded sexual male; he oozed sexuality, unlike any other man she'd met. She figured, with just the two of them staying in this house together, they'd end up in bed sooner or later. She had to consider, was she ready for that?

And the answer was yes. Even if it was just for the experience. Maybe a reacquaintance, to see if it was as good as she remembered. She smiled. He'd love that. "Let's go to bed to see if we're still as good as we were."

She shook her head. So not happening.

She bounded off the bed, dressed in clean clothes, brushed her hair back, putting it into a single braid down her back, grabbed a sweater, and walked downstairs.

And of course he was already up, drinking coffee at the kitchen table.

"Did you go to bed?" she asked as she poured herself a cup. She turned to the table and sat down beside him.

"I did."

"Did you find anything in the computer last night?"

He shook his head. "Nothing's shown up yet. I wasn't really expecting it to, but I needed to make sure."

She understood and appreciated the thoroughness.

"Any update on Anna and what was his name? ... Flynn?"

He nodded with a smile. "Apparently the two are slamming sparks off each other."

She thought about it and shook her head. "I wish I was a fly on the wall. It would be great entertainment."

He studied her. "Looks like you had a good night's sleep."

"Like a baby," she announced with a smile. "What's on the agenda for today?"

He let her lead the conversation as they discussed their shopping to be done—what groceries they wanted to pick up and any other household items they might need.

Just the thought of all that food made her hungry. She

got up and opened the fridge, brought out some of the treats Alfred had packed for them. She didn't want any of it to go to waste.

Together they munched through their breakfast as they made plans. With the sun shining outside, it would be another glorious day. She found no lake with her search for local things to do, but she'd love to go for a swim.

"Is there a place to go swimming around here?"

"There could be a few rivers but not in the immediate area. Not within walking distance."

"Okay. Maybe another day."

"We'll be staying within walking distance for the week," he said. "At least until we see if there's any repercussions from all the mail outs."

She froze. "I forgot they went out yesterday." She stared out the window blindly. "It could take them two or three days to go across the country."

"Levi's already getting phone calls, because, don't forget, everything went out digitally first."

"Great. So, then what?"

"People have to sort through the information, verify its validity, and then start the rounds of interviews and tie up the evidence." He gave her a reassuring smile. "The journalist is ferreting out more information, and the DA has requested a meeting with Levi. It's all moving. Let time do its thing."

She nodded. "We're dreaming if we think we'll be here only one week, right?"

"Stay positive. Now that the right people have the information, we need them to act."

"That's one of the things I learned about life. Just because someone does something, it doesn't mean the rest of the world has the same idea."

He smiled at her. "And we have nothing better to do than spend the week here and enjoy it. So let's head back downtown and get some shopping done."

She stood and grabbed the dishes off the table. As she washed them, he grabbed a tea towel and quickly dried the dishes, putting them away. Another ten minutes and they were walking out the front door.

She stopped on the doorstep and looked at the neighborhood, a big hill rising behind their nice house nestled into the bush with the driveway heading straight toward the road. She wanted to go for a walk by herself a little later. When he stepped beside her, they headed down the driveway and back on the pathway to town.

"Can we stop by Freddy's?"

He nodded. "Every day if you want."

"Okay. Routines are good for me."

She linked her hand with his, and they chatted about seemingly useless stuff. But, to her, they gave her an insight into who he was. She talked about flowers, talked about animals—getting his view on animal shelters for Anna's sake—and talked about food. She learned he absolutely adored steak. He was male. He also had a sweet tooth for homemade apple pie, and he was a mean cook of Creole food, a skill handed down from his grandma. They discussed a few dishes they might buy the ingredients for and would cook later. By the time they walked into the grocery store, she was feeling very much like they were partners. Certainly good friends.

That set the pattern. Every morning they got up, had breakfast and coffee, figured out what to buy for their dinner and walked to the stores in town. They went out for lunch sometimes, and occasionally they stopped for coffee in the small café. Every day they stopped in to see Freddy. So far everything was good.

On the morning of the fourth day, she got up to find heavy clouds and rain. "Phooey." But she dressed just a little warmer and walked downstairs.

Instead of seeing Merk at the kitchen table in his usual spot, coffee in hand, she had to track him down in the office. "Problems?"

"Movement," he said. "The DA's office is busy picking up various members of the company."

"Oh, that's excellent," she said with joy in her voice. "Maybe this will be over sooner than later."

"Not necessarily." He looked at her and said, "Don't forget they have to have more than just what you gave for proof. But they have agents with search warrants at the company right now. So, with any luck, they can check some of these files."

"I have log-ins and passwords," she offered immediately. "I never thought to give them to you earlier as I'd already given you all the information I had accessed with them."

He froze and turned toward her. "Pardon?"

"Remember, I have a photographic memory," she said. "I can give them passwords, file names, and the log-ins." She shrugged. "I can't say it's for everything, but it's what I have, and maybe it'll help them get access."

She sat down, and he tossed a pad of paper at her. She carefully wrote down everything she could remember about all the log-ins she'd seen and used. When she handed her list back to him, he immediately typed it up.

She walked into the kitchen to grab another coffee. Her mood was good. It might be dark and gray outside, but this was progress, and she was happy with that. She filled her cup and went back to the office. Realizing his cup was empty, she went to get him a refill. By time she returned, he was cross-referencing what she'd written to what he'd typed.

"I'm sending this off to Levi and Ice. They can forward it to the DA's office." Then he leaned back and looked at her. "That's done now. Hopefully that'll help them get the information they need." He picked up the coffee cup and held it up to her. "Thanks for this."

"No problem," she said. "So now the routine day-to-day thing?"

"To a certain extent. We'll check in with Freddy. Then maybe, instead of grocery shopping, we could have lunch at that French place he talked about."

She nodded. "I slept late, so I'm not terribly hungry for breakfast."

She finally realized how late it was when she got up to refill her third cup of coffee and saw the time on the coffee-pot. No wonder he hadn't been in the kitchen waiting for her. She was an hour later than usual. But she also had good news to share. She turned and said, "I heard from my uncle. He sent me a text saying he was in California at a friend's, and he was fine." She beamed. "So one less person to worry about."

"Excellent. I'm sorry about the rest of your family not being close."

"Definitely not an easy way to grow up. There were no constants. Nothing to count on. It surprised me when I married you so fast. Then, when it instantly fell apart, it seemed like a repeat of my life. Something I thought would be there, wasn't." She gave him a quiet smile. "Live and learn."

"Learning to trust is huge," he said quietly. "I've been

147

dealing with that a lot this last year in my work. But it bleeds into other parts of our lives even though we do our best not to let it. Still, we have to begin somewhere."

"So are we starting here—with us?" she asked abruptly. "Are we really looking at a relationship together? One where we can count on each other?"

"I'd like that," he said with a smile. "Is that why you didn't tell anyone about your photographic memory?"

She nodded. "Growing up, my siblings hated me for it. Anytime I used it, they'd get me into trouble. So I struggled with that along with that whole 'who is going to be there for me' thing."

He finished his coffee and stood, saying, "How about we head downtown? By the time we're done, we should be ready for an early lunch."

"That works for me." She filled the coffee cups with soapy water to soak while they were gone, turned off the pot, and waited at the door for him. She already had her sweater on. It was just that kind of a day. When he joined her, he took one last look around, double-checked that everything was locked, then wrapped an arm around her shoulders. "Let's go."

HE DIDN'T KNOW how truly perceptive she was, like, if she had noticed he double-checked the locks in the office, the kitchen, and then the front door. She probably understood they had entered a very different phase now—where people understood what kind of information she'd brought to life.

The truth was, things had started the day before yesterday, but only now was the word getting out to the public. Levi had called to warn them, not that Merk needed the heads-up. He knew how dangerous this next step was. They were all looking out for her. His job was to ensure no one found her.

So far his brother hadn't called. He'd take that as a good sign.

"First stop is Freddy's."

"Okay," she said amiably.

He really liked that about her. She knew when to follow orders, and apparently she also knew when to tell him off for giving orders. He grinned at the reminder of their conversation a few nights before.

As they walked down the street, the clouds above looked like they would dump on them.

"We should have brought umbrellas."

"I don't have any," he admitted. "We may have to stop in for coffee before lunch."

But they made it to the store before the rain came down. As they walked into the gloomy storefront, she asked, "Does he ever clean out here?"

"That would bring customers in," he said drily. "I don't think he wants anything to do with that."

That got a laugh out of her.

He tapped on the bell on the front counter and waited for Freddy to come out. But, when Merk had no sign of Freddy, Merk hit the bell several more times. The old guy could be in the bathroom.

When still no answer came, he held a finger to his lips and whispered, "Stay here."

He walked to the beaded curtain and peered through it. He couldn't see anything because of the boxes in the doorway. He would have to move them, and that would give away his position. Damn.

Moving as fast as he could, he slipped behind and stayed low as he snuck past the boxes, to the point where the room opened up in front of him. Freddy had it arranged so nobody could see anything until they reached the center of his big electronic shop. The monitors were off. He checked out the back room further, in case Freddy had collapsed on the floor from a heart attack, but no sign of him was anywhere.

He frowned. Merk walked back to the front of the store and brought Katina into the back room with him. "It's unlike him to step out of the store."

"He has to go home sometime," she said calmly. "Maybe he's gone for an early lunch himself."

Merk nodded. "Anything's possible." But as he continued to prowl the room, Merk walked past the back door, slightly ajar. He pushed it open and stepped out to check the alleyway—and froze. He'd just found Freddy, dead beside the Dumpster.

Merk needed to check things out here, but he didn't want her inside alone. With this new development, he turned and called in a low voice, "Katina, come here." When she walked out to him, he grabbed her hand and tucked her up close. That's when she saw the body.

She slapped a hand over her mouth. "Oh, no," she cried softly. "Did he die of natural causes?" she whispered into her hand with hope.

He walked over to study the body. As he got closer, he could see the blood pooling underneath his face. Because of a slight incline to the alley, the blood ran underneath the Dumpster. Now that Merk was close enough, he could see the gunshot wound at the temple.

"Damn." He turned to look at Katina and said, "He's

been shot."

She immediately stepped back to hug the door, her hand still over her mouth, staring at him wordlessly. He'd seen way too much in his life to be surprised by anything, but he hated to see this happen to Freddy. He was one of the good guys.

Immediately a gun fired close by and hit the metal Dumpster beside them. Instantly the sound of racing footsteps receded.

Merk bolted back inside, dragging Katina with him. He shoved her behind the desks and raced to the side of the door and peered out, weapon ready.

The alley was empty. Then it had been empty before.

Shit. He turned back to her. "Stay here. I'll do a quick sweep of the area. Stay hidden. I won't be long." With a hard look to make sure she understood, he waited for her response. She quickly nodded and slipped farther out of sight. Good thing. He slipped outside and raced in the direction the footsteps had gone. As Freddy's was the last store on the block, Merk peered around the corner but found nothing. He could feel that the asshole was gone, but he couldn't prove it. He tucked the gun under his shirt and quickly walked to the front of the block, searching for a likely killer.

Nothing.

Back at the store he stepped into the entrance from the alley and called out, "Katina?"

"Here." She stepped from her hiding place and raced into his arms.

"You're safe. He's long gone." Holding her close, Merk pulled out his phone and called Levi. When he answered, Merk gave him the details. Much swearing followed on the other end.

"Okay, I'll phone his boss and let them know. You call the local police and get that in progress."

"I can do that." After Merk hung up, he turned to Katina. "I have to call the police. In the meantime, Levi'll contact Freddy's company."

A frown line formed between her brows. "Freddy's company?"

Merk nodded. "Freddy was part of a network. We'll see what ends up happening to the store after this."

"And does that mean whoever killed him saw all that he was keeping an eye on?" she asked nervously. "Is Anna safe? Are we safe?"

"In this situation, we have to assume the worst," he said quietly. "Let me call the police, then I have to take care of the shop."

She stared at him from the doorway, her gaze going from inside to outside, and said, "But, if the police come here, they'll know what he was doing too, won't they?"

"Yes. That's something the company will have to deal with."

She turned to look inside again. "We should shut everything down then?"

He hesitated for a moment, then said, "Let's do that first, in case the police get here in the next five minutes."

She frowned at him. "There won't actually be any police in a small town like this, will there? Wouldn't they have to come from the closest city?"

He nodded. "I suspect so."

"We can't leave him lying out there like that for the flies."

Just then his phone rang. It was Levi. "I called the cops myself. They are sending an officer down this afternoon, probably take an hour and a half. Can you cover up the body to hide it from passersby?"

Merk nodded. "We were just working on that." And then he spied a series of boxes. "I can cover him up with cardboard. But if anybody comes back here, it's going to look suspicious."

"Take pictures now. Then cover him up and wait until the police and the forensics team get there."

"Okay, got it."

Merk took a few pictures with his cell phone, then walked back inside to look for something better to cover Freddy with. On the back of the door was an old blanket. He took it out and carefully covered the old man. Then using the boxes, he built up a wall around him. At least for the short term, it might keep the general public from seeing him. When Merk turned around, he found Katina, standing in the open doorway, tears in her eyes.

"It doesn't seem fair. He was a good man. He didn't deserve this."

"The hard fact of life is nobody deserves this," Merk said as he calmly ushered her back inside. "We'll keep an eye on him until the police arrive. According to Levi, that should be about ninety minutes. In the meantime, we have things to do here."

He systematically went through the back room and shut down all the machines. Then he carefully moved all the tables against the one wall, so they were all stacked up, as if not in use. He brought two more tables over, setting them up with some of the dusty old equipment from the front shelves, placing them in a way that made it look like Freddy was doing some repairs. Merk also remembered to lock the front door and to switch the sign from Open to Closed.

He turned back to her and said, "Now to wait."

She glanced down at her watch. "It's already been forty-five minutes. They could be here anytime."

He nodded and took one last glance around the place, hating that now they would be blind everywhere, and led her to the alleyway. "I'd feel better if I stand guard out back," he said. "I don't want to leave him alone."

She smiled mistily up at him. "Nobody should be left alone like this."

Chapter 15

WHEN THE POLICE finally arrived, she found them both efficient and cold. Not only did they not know the victim, they didn't know the town. At least not very well. They asked a few questions, which she and Merk answered easily, then they were ushered out of the way.

Merk grabbed her hand and told the officer they were heading to the little French restaurant in town for lunch.

By the look on the guys' faces, Katina didn't think they had heard Merk.

Although she wasn't hungry, she knew she needed to eat because they didn't know what they were facing now. The curtain of safety had just been ripped away. They'd entered a whole new ball game.

As they walked away from the alley, she said, "Worst case scenario, we have to assume we've been found. One of those monitors showed the house we were staying in."

He nodded and, in a low voice, said, "But, unless they happen to be locals, they wouldn't know where it was."

"Yet it wouldn't take much to ask a local," she countered. "Everybody would know."

Again he nodded.

When they got to the restaurant, he pushed open the door, and the two of them entered. The place was half full, and they took a seat in the back. A waitress with a big smile handed them menus.

Katina studied it but didn't see anything that appealed. He didn't even open his. She placed hers on top of his and said, "Good. Order whatever you want for both of us. I'll be in the bathroom."

She got up and walked back to the ladies' room, a small single room. She locked the door, hung her purse on the wall hook, and just stood, staring at herself in the mirror.

What a hell of a morning. She was so damn sad about Freddy. She lifted her hands, saw her fingers tremble. What the hell would they do now? Turning on the hot water, she briskly washed her face and then turned the water to cold, wet a paper towel, and patted it on her cheeks. She had to get a grip. Events weren't going back to the way they had been. She'd had her vacation. She'd had a few days of an idyllic lifestyle—a few days to forget. But that was it.

The reality of the situation stared back at her. People were being killed over the information she'd found.

She used the facilities, washed her hands once again, then grabbed her purse, and walked out to the larger room. She couldn't stop looking around this time because anybody in this restaurant could have killed that nice old man. At least, she told herself, the way he'd been shot, she doubted he'd suffered much.

Sitting at the table once again, she leaned forward and said, "Do you think he walked outside willingly, or was he at gunpoint?"

"I don't think it was willingly."

She nodded. "Did he shut off the monitors? They weren't on when we went in."

He looked at her and smiled. "I wondered if you noticed that."

"Do you think he knew?"

"Fred was a canny old codger who was wise in the ways of the world. I think he had some idea he might be in trouble."

She wondered why she hadn't seen it before. "I'm not cut out for this," she said. "It's only just now I wondered."

"Don't worry about it. Stress will do strange things to you."

She realized the menus were gone and in their place were two steaming cups of coffee. She cradled her cup gratefully. "What did you order?"

He said, his gaze intent on sending texts, "It's a surprise. Wait and see."

She nodded and had to be satisfied with that.

Finally the waitress returned and set down two plates full of crepes.

Katina grinned. "Oh, this looks wonderful. Thank you."

The waitress beamed, left, and returned with a big bowl of whipping cream and another of fresh blueberries. As she turned to walk away again, she said, "Help yourself to both, dear."

Nobody needed to tell Katina twice. She split the blueberries between her and Merk's plates, then dumped liberal splotches of whipping cream on top both. And still he didn't lift his face from his phone. She kicked him lightly under the table. He lifted his head and frowned at her. She nodded toward the plate at his side and said, "Eat."

He glanced at it and put his phone down. "Well, this looks lovely." He pulled it toward him, and then there was silence.

As soon as they finished, she knew they'd be leaving. What she didn't know was if they were actually leaving the house too. Because she hadn't been terribly smart.

She hadn't left everything packed, ready to run. In fact she'd unpacked everything and made herself at home. That thinking had come to a sudden, irrefutable end. She needed at least a half hour to collect all her stuff again. Foolish. If they were going home to something very ugly, she wouldn't have that much time.

Mentally she sorted through the items she had sprawled out, figuring out what she would take if she only had a few seconds.

By the time they paid and were walking outside, she realized that, if they were going home, they were going a different route. "Are we hiding our tracks?"

"Not necessarily, but we're climbing up the ridge to look down at the house. We're not walking toward the house like we normally do because, if anybody's watching, they'd see us before we made them."

"Right. I'll pack up as soon as we get home."

He nodded. "Good, it's for the best."

Her shoulders sagged for a long moment, then she bolstered herself with the knowledge that, so far, she was alive. Fred hadn't had that option. "It is what it is."

"That's my girl." He reached out and caught her hand as they climbed up the hill behind the house.

Once there, he dropped her hand and took the lead. She was in good shape, but she wasn't in fantastic shape. Merk was definitely in fantastic shape. He slowed his pace so she could keep up. By the time they made it to the crest of the hill, she was huffing and puffing.

He led her across the top of the ridge and then crouched, telling her, "Stay as low as you can."

And again she wasn't anywhere near as graceful as he

was, but she crouched down and kept moving fairly low.

Finally they came to the spot where they could look down on the property. Instead of him standing there, staring, he actually sat down cross-legged and waited. She joined him. "What are we waiting for?"

But he didn't answer; instead he studied the layout. She realized they would not be leaving this ridge until he was sure it was safe. In truth, she agreed with that, but she didn't know how long it would take. So she settled back to wait.

They didn't have to wait long. Forty minutes later, during which she'd shifted her position a couple times while Merk sat still at her side, she saw somebody come out the back door and stand on the small deck. She froze. The man's gaze never lifted to where they sat. He did a quick search, then turned and walked back into the house.

In a furious whisper, she said, "Who the hell was that?"

His voice low and deadly, Merk answered, "I'd guess the man who killed Freddy."

MERK LAUGHED INWARDLY at her inability to sit still. She probably thought she was doing really well in that department, but then she'd fidgeted with her fingers and hands. She had straightened her legs, then tucked them underneath, even rocked back and forth.

Whereas he'd been quite capable of sitting and just resting in a moment of stillness. He had had enough practice at it. His training had been brutal. As he sat, he considered. The man he'd seen, was he alone? And why had he come out on the back porch? There was no need for that. Merk wished he had his binoculars with him, then he would have a better idea of who all was in the house. As it was, Merk and Katina would have to creep back down the way they'd come and wait until dark to sneak into the house.

Just as he made that decision, a vehicle drove up the driveway. He frowned as it disappeared around the front of the house. He didn't recognize the truck. A few minutes later the vehicle backed out and turned, disappearing down the street toward the village. One man had driven in; two men had left.

Did that mean the house was empty? Or had he left bugs and camera equipment in lieu of manpower?

Merk had choices to make. But the outcome of those choices could be deadly. He didn't want Katina anywhere close to the place. He needed to go in and check it out himself.

Had they taken anything? His laptop was there, but he'd put it away in the drawer. Depended on how well they had searched the place.

He turned to her. "Where's your laptop?"

"I was watching a movie on it last night," she said, "so it was on the bed." She shrugged. "I was just thinking today, after we found Freddy, how lax I got and left my stuff everywhere." She looked over at him. "Do we need to stay here on this hill?"

"I want *you* to stay here," he said. "I'll slip down and see if the house is empty."

"And if it isn't? Can you handle one intruder, ... two intruders?"

He nodded. "That's no problem. The problem is whether they left bugs behind and/or a security system or video camera feed. If they had an hour, that would've been long enough to set up something simple. And we've been in town enough to get noticed. That's an automatic reason to check."

"I guess the neighbors would know the house wasn't empty."

"It's not as much the neighbors, because, as you can see, nobody is close, but the villagers always know." He studied her face intently. "You're okay to stay here?"

She nodded. He leaned over and kissed her hard on the lips. "I'll be back."

At that, she said, "You promise?"

"I promise."

At a light run he went down the hill, staying away from the rocks in his path. He didn't stop to look behind where he'd left her. He kept his eye on the house and on the windows, in case anybody saw him. With the momentum he had going, he used it to swing himself up onto the porch where the man had stepped out. There were stairs on the side, but he didn't want to do the expected.

He landed lightly and pressed against the wall, waiting to see if the door would open. But no sound could be heard from the inside. He tested the door and found it unlocked. He pushed it open and slipped inside. He stopped just inside the entrance and listened. As far as he could tell, the house was empty, had a hollow echo to it.

He looked up in the hallway and searched for camera feeds. They could be hard to find, depending on how well hidden they were. He presumed they actually had that kind of equipment. The men had to confirm Katina was here, and then they could come back with more men.

He moved through the lower floor and found nothing missing, nothing disturbed. Which was interesting in itself. Had they searched the place? At the office door he stopped, and it looked relatively undisturbed. He found his laptop still inside the bottom drawer where he'd left it. Then again it had a mechanism underneath to open it, and it didn't look like a drawer.

None of this was by chance. They'd spent a lifetime dealing with this kind of stuff. Even the furniture had been picked out for such reasons. He moved swiftly to the base of the stairs and crept up to the top floor.

One swift pass let him know the place was empty. He checked Katina's room first. She was right. Discarded clothing, blankets, and tossed pillows were all around her room. Not a mess but it was in disarray. However, it didn't look like anything had been searched. But a woman obviously was staying here. She had her purse on her, so nothing was left behind to identify the woman was Katina.

Except her laptop. He'd deal with that later.

He hadn't seen any sign of cameras up to this point. But he didn't trust it. It felt like somebody had been completely through the place. And that wasn't good. He walked over to his room with that same sense of somebody having been here. Also not good. If there were cameras, he couldn't afford to be seen.

At the closet, he pulled a pillowcase off the shelf and, with his pocketknife, quickly cut two holes and pulled it over his head. Then he walked into her room casually. Calmly and efficiently he packed up all her stuff. She'd brought two bags, and, sure enough, both were well stuffed by the time he was done. He made the bed and cleaned up the bathroom of toiletries, then carried the bags to the top of stairs and picked up his already packed bag. On a mission he was never anything but ready.

Carrying everything downstairs, including her laptop, he walked over to the office and grabbed his laptop. With one last look around, he headed to the kitchen, then to the back door. They had often walked out from here. He laid the bags and the laptop on the back porch and turned to look up at her, and waved, letting her know all was okay.

In the kitchen he pulled out Alfred's basket from the closet and proceeded to quickly pack up everything they had that was edible. The rest he threw in the garbage and secured the trash bag. They'd have to drop it down the road. He had no time to dispose of it right now.

The keys to the truck were hidden in it, and the vehicle was in the garage. He headed back to the porch, grabbed the bags, carried them down the stairs and opened up the garage door, thankful the truck was still here. Using up valuable time, he dumped what he was carrying into the back, opened the glove box, pulled out a tester, and quickly scanned the vehicle. When it came up clean, he raced inside for the rest of their belongings. By the time he had cleaned up the rest of the garbage he'd left, she stood at the bottom of the hill. Furious he turned to her and snapped, "I told you to stay there."

"And yet you waved. I thought that meant everything was okay." She shrugged. "I was wondering if you needed to pack up anything." She stopped and looked at him. "Why are you wearing that?"

He frowned and then realized she was referring to the pillowcase. He pulled it off his head and said, "Damn it. Get into the truck. We're done."

"Should I take a last look and see if you forgot anything? Did you grab all my clothes, toiletries, and my laptop?"

He nodded. "Unless you hid anything?"

Instantly she shook her head. "No, I promise."

He motioned toward the truck. "Get in."

He pulled the pillowcase back over his head and walked

through the house one last time, then quickly locked all the doors. Back at the garage, he hopped into the truck, took off the pillowcase again, and cranked the engine. And realized she was no longer sitting inside.

He bolted from the truck and raced around to the passenger side.

To see a man holding a gun to her throat.

Merk swore like the sailor he was. Where the hell had that asshole come from?

"Stay where you are, and she won't get hurt."

"Like hell," Katina said bitterly. "You'll kill me, like you did Freddy."

"Not if you're good." He pulled her back toward the side door leading to the yard, likely the way he'd come in after seeing Katina come down the hill.

"Piss off," she snapped and slammed her elbow into his gut, spinning and jamming his gun up toward the ceiling. A shot went off.

Merk was on him in two seconds, and the asshole was on the floor, out cold. Merk snagged Katina into his arms and buried his face in her neck. "Dear God, I could have lost you."

She was crying uncontrollably against his chest. He'd have done anything to save her from this. He gave her a moment, then gently moved her to the truck's passenger door. It was even more important to get the hell out now.

And easier to lift her up than to get her to let go. Finally he untangled her arms from around his neck.

"We have to leave before he comes to or his buddies return, but first I need to find out who this man is."

She nodded and swiped at her teary eyes.

He dropped to the unconscious man and emptied his

pockets. Opening the wallet, Merk found the man's driver's license with a matching photo, cash, and several credit cards all pointing to the man being Samuel Cheevers.

"Let me see," she whispered, now beside him. "You called Levi?"

Good idea. He dumped the bits and pieces in her lap and stepped back to take a picture of the man. He quickly sent that to Levi and followed up with an even faster phone call.

When he was done, Katina handed back the man's belongings and said, "There's no point in keeping his wallet."

Levi tossed it on the ground beside the man, then walked to the driver's side of the truck. By now a sense of urgency was riding him—hard.

All of this had taken too long. If the asshole's buddies were coming back, they were likely on the way. So Merk and Katina would be caught leaving. He made it outside the garage, hit the button to close the door, hiding the prone man inside, then slowly drove down the driveway, and took the corner. He headed in the opposite direction of the truck he'd seen earlier and gunned it.

With any luck they'd made it free and clear. But he didn't live in a world of luck. He usually found he had to make his own because damn little of it was handed out for free.

Chapter 16

S HE WONDERED HOW long it would take for her to relax enough to realize they were safe. Merk had been driving like a crazy man for an hour already, and she kept looking behind to see if they were followed. It would be a long time before she forgot the sensation of someone holding a gun to her. Still she'd gotten free, and Merk had taken him down.

She could be proud of that.

Yet tension coiled in her stomach like a snake ready to take her out.

Finally she forced herself to relax by practicing a few deep-breathing techniques.

"Feeling better?" Merk asked, his voice calm and quiet as it floated through the truck. He was obviously used to dealing with this kind of nightmare.

"I am, a little bit, yes."

"Nice job back there."

"Thanks. We made a good team," she admitted. "You don't realize just how badly your muscles are knotted until you try to unknot them. Where are we going now?"

"Another house, different state."

And that was all he offered. It really didn't matter. As long as nobody was shooting at them, she was good. The thought of being separated from Merk right now was terrifying. He was big, solid, a dependable barrier between her and those nasty assholes.

"How long do you think before we're safe?"

"No idea. Levi's dealing with the DA. They have to round everybody up and see how far the poison goes. These kinds of crimes can involve dozens of people." He took his eyes off the road to glance her way. "And he had the local police check out the Samuel Cheevers we left behind, but he was gone."

"Of course he was." Maybe they should have killed him after all. "The police don't care about the little guys," she said. "What they really want is the big fish." She reached up to rub her temple where the gunman had hit her. Between the stitches on her leg and the bruise on her temple, she would be a mess before she got home again. Wherever home would end up being.

"Depends if the little guys did the killing. Even if the big fish ordered them, the little fish are the ones who did the deed."

Right. Eloise and Freddy. And, of course, her own kidnapping and today's incident. Knowing they would be driving for a few hours, she curled up into the corner of the truck and tried to sleep.

Her phone buzzed. She checked the ID. It was Anna. "Is there any chance of my phone causing the trouble?"

"Not likely. Was that a text or email that just came in?"

"A text from Anna." She read the message and chuckled. "She doesn't appreciate Flynn. Wants him to get lost and wants to know how long before she can boot this guy out of her life."

Merk laughed. "That sounds like Flynn."

"So is it safe to answer?"

He glanced at her. "Yes."

She set about answering the text, careful to not say anything important, and adding that Flynn was a really good guy. Anna just had to get used to him.

Her response came back within seconds.

No getting used to this jerk.

Katina really hated that she had put Anna in this situation, but it was for her own good, and, if Merk said Flynn was a good guy, then she trusted him. Anna wasn't the easiest person either. She tended to be way too passionate and emphatic about everything in her world. And her world revolved around saving animals.

Hours later Katina sat up with interest as Merk slowed the vehicle and turned off the main highway. She rubbed the sleep from her eyes and realized she'd just missed a sign. He drove for another ten or fifteen minutes, then took a dirt road. Frowning she watched, peering through the windshield into the near darkness. "This time we're really off the main road."

"Absolutely. Doesn't get much more rustic than this."

She hoped it wasn't too rustic. She still liked a few modern amenities, like running water. But if staying alive meant doing without, then that was fine too.

When he finally came to a stop, it was in front of a small log cabin. He hopped from the truck, grabbed a flashlight from behind the seat, and came around to help her down. Normally she got out on her own, but she could see she would need help here as there was no pathway. He led the way up to the front step. She could now see it wasn't so much a log cabin but a rustic cabin with some planking for sides. While she studied the outside, he opened the door. And she realized he must have a hidden key somewhere. She just hadn't seen him look for it. No way he could have known they would go to all these places before they left. Or had he?

If he actually had planned for that level of problems, she wondered what else was planned.

Inside was wooden furniture and a fireplace with the wood stacked on the side. She wondered again if it had modern amenities. She was relieved when he hit a light switch, and low ambient light shone from above.

"I haven't been here in a while. I always liked this place though."

Merk walked into another room, and she followed on his heels. A kitchen with a fridge. He opened the fridge door to find it recently fully stocked.

Instantly her mood lifted. "I see you have helpers all over the place."

"We do at that."

"But does that mean the more people who know about this place, the more dangerous it is for everyone?"

"Nobody knows we're here. Just because the fridge was stocked, it doesn't mean anybody has a clue who's coming."

She considered that and realized he was right. If this was a rental cabin option, services like shopping were often supplied for the new arrivals. And who knew who was arriving because the whole point was peace and quiet and privacy.

Katina waited inside, studying the big fireplace, wondering if she knew actually how to light a fire while he walked out to the truck and brought in their luggage. She decided that her camping days weren't so far behind her, and maybe she could handle this.

She crumpled up some paper that was off to the side,

then opened the flue. Using the kindling, she got a small blaze going. She was actually feeling pretty cheeky and proud of herself as she stood and watched the wood catch fire. By the time Merk was done, she had layered a few bigger logs on top.

He came over to stand beside her. "Nice job. I was getting to that next."

And then the coffeemaker beeped. She realized he'd put on coffee while she'd been making the fire.

With a big grin she said, "We make a great pair."

He held out his arms, and she ran into them, grateful for the hug. He held her close. "We absolutely do. I know you're worried about all this, but we will only be here for a few days, maybe a week, and then will move on again."

She nodded her head, gently rocking against his chest. "Thank you for looking after me so well," she whispered.

"Ha. If I was looking after you, you can bet you would never have seen Freddy's body, and you wouldn't have been scared out of your mind when the intruders went into the house or then pointed a gun at your throat."

"But it's okay. We got away, and who knows where the hell they are now." She tilted her head back and looked at him. "I hate to say it, but I'm hungry."

He dropped a kiss on the tip of her nose and said, "I was expecting that actually. I'm surprised you made it all the way through the trip without asking for Alfred's basket."

"Then I shall go to the fridge." She stepped from his arms and opened the refrigerator door to explore. Beside her, he studied the contents and asked, "What do you want?"

"Sandwiches are fast so I vote for those." She reached into the fridge and pulling out the fixings.

Two kinds of meat, cheese, lettuce, tomatoes, and onions. He found a loaf of fresh bread and brought it over. Between the two of them, they found the rest of the things they needed, like a knife for slicing the bread, onions, and tomatoes. Soon they were sitting in front of the fire, which was now blazed happily, munching on sandwiches.

"How late is it?" She looked at her phone that she'd left on the table.

"It's after 8:00 p.m."

She nodded. "I suppose the bedrooms are upstairs, but, if it's not any warmer there, I vote we sleep in front of the fire."

"There are small heaters if we need them. But I don't believe there's a central furnace."

She shook her head. "How is that possible in this day and age? It obviously gets very cold here."

"Remember that request that you bring something warm?"

And that answered her previous question. "You planned to come here anyway?"

"Sure, this is our second spot on the route."

"Route?" She studied his face in the flickering shadows. They sat together on the same couch, and she was close enough to see the reflection in his eyes as the flames flickered and danced in the fireplace.

He explained, "We have to have several spots close and available, so I made a circular route that would eventually take us back home to the compound when and if it is safe to go."

"When and if?" she said, her voice rising. "Please tell me this won't be a long-term issue."

"It's possible," he admitted. "But we can't focus on that. You set something into motion, and we're dealing the best we can with the fallout."

Right. That put it back in perspective again. She slumped in place. "Well, I don't have a job I'll miss out on, but I can't just spend the next few months staying undercover without doing something," she said.

"We'll make do," he said cheerfully. "Let's not worry about the time frame. It's not even been a week yet."

She nodded. "Is anybody else likely to know this is the second place on your route?"

"Not to worry," he said.

"Does anybody else know about this place?" She studied his face. "If the truck and our phones weren't tracked, then nobody knows where the hell we are?"

"The only people who know our location are Levi, Ice, and the rest of the team." He tucked himself up against the corner of the couch and, with a gentle nudge, pulled her against his chest. "Relax. We'll get to spend a week in the woods, just the two of us."

Was it her imagination, or was a little hint of an innuendo in there? Or maybe a question to see how she would react? Inside she smiled. Because, damn, if one thing sounded really good right now, it was a week away in complete isolation. Just the two of them. Small towns were great, but this was going be a completely different experience.

As far she was concerned, it was time to get back to their relationship, whatever that meant. And what a great time to find out what was developing between them. It would happen either upstairs in the bed or down here in front of the fireplace. She didn't plan on leaving his side. And, no, not because she was scared, but because this man had been driving her crazy for a long time. She knew how good they were together. She just wanted a chance to find out all over again.

She shifted her position so she could raise herself up. She leaned forward and kissed his cheek. "A week together sounds perfect."

He turned and studied her face in the shadows. She could see the question in his gaze. But she held back her smile. She wanted to see if he would make a move. Or if she had to. Of course he was on the job, whereas she wasn't. She actually had no compunction about leading him down the wrong path, if that's what was holding him back.

With his free hand he slowly stroked her cheek, letting his thumb move across her lips. She kissed it, nibbling ever-so-slightly. When he raised one eyebrow, she smiled. He cupped her chin and tilted it toward him, then leaned forward and gave her a gentle kiss.

HE HAD TO admit, this was in the back of his mind when he realized they were coming here. He'd wondered about taking her to bed in the last place, but she hadn't settled down enough. And there'd been enough to do to keep their minds busy. Besides it had been fun watching their relationship grow and deepen. The little teasing glances and tantalizing looks. They were both heading for this moment. And now, on a couch in front of the fireplace, it was damn hard not to think it was the perfect moment.

He deepened the kiss, loving when she threw her arms around his neck and kissed him back. He crushed her against his chest, remembering how her passionate responses got to him the last time. They'd spent hours in bed, tumbling across the sheets, enjoying being so perfectly matched. He didn't expect this to be any different.

"Upstairs or here?"

She eased back, a slightly muddled look in her eyes that he loved. He dropped a kiss on her nose and, not wanting to let go of the taste of her, did it again and then again. He ended up exploring her entire face, kissing her eyelids, her cheeks, before finding her lips again.

She still hadn't answered. And he realized, chances were, they wouldn't make it to the bedroom. As far as space went, he wasn't sure a short couch was the best answer either.

He shifted her to sit beside him. He got up quickly, moved the coffee table out of the way, pulled her to her feet, and took her over by the fireplace. He took the big cushions off the couch, laid them in front of the fireplace, and stepped back to wait. Her gaze went from the fireplace to the makeshift mattress, then back to him again.

"I do love resourcefulness." In a surprise move, she kicked off her shoes, took off her socks, and then her sweater.

And stripped right down to her skin. She stood completely comfortable in her nakedness, shadows dancing across her hills and valleys. He was stunned by her natural beauty. He never really had a chance to see her in Vegas. Not like this. She stepped onto the mattress and took another step toward him.

"Aren't you a little overdressed?"

That galvanized him into action. He sat to pull off his boots and socks, yanked his shirt over his head. By the time he reached for his belt buckle, he was already hard and ready. He managed to open his belt buckle before she slipped her hands inside his jeans, and further progress undressing came to a complete halt. He leaned his head back, barely holding inside his groans as she caressed the tip of him.

In a thick voice he said, "If you keep that up, it'll be over before we start."

Her fingers undid the snap on his jeans and lowered the zipper. She said, "As I seem to remember, it was never very long before you were ready for round two." Slipping her hands inside his underwear, she dropped them down past his hips and followed them on her knees.

Jesus. He could barely step out of his clothes with her hands so eagerly exploring him. As he drew his hands through her hair, watching her, he thought he'd never seen anything more beautiful. She had a complete lack of self-consciousness that was lovely. She was content in who she was as a person. When her lips closed around the tip of his erection, a groan ripped free. Taking her wandering hands, he stepped back and shifted her until she laid the full length of the mattress. He dropped down beside her before she could scramble back to her knees.

He tugged her hands over her head to hold them still and lowered his mouth, kissing her like he'd been wanting to do for days, weeks it seemed. No way this would be over so fast. He wouldn't let it. He'd been looking forward to it for a long time. And the memory of what they'd had together had haunted him for even longer.

Because, although she'd laughed at the idea, he *had* thought about *what if?* ... He had thought about what if they'd actually given it a try? And he'd worried and wondered.

He had said that getting married was a mistake. But he had often considered if leaving her the next day had been the bigger mistake. At the time it seemed like nothing so perfect, so wonderful, could've been a mistake. So when he had walked away, … he'd questioned his sanity.

When he left the military, he'd thought again about this, but he didn't put any time and effort into renewing his contact with her. He figured she'd moved on.

But, of course, she'd been just as busy as he had. They hadn't found time to reconnect. But he always knew he wanted to, in the back of his mind. Here he had a chance to prove to her they belonged together.

Because, if he'd learned anything, this last week or so had shown him that they'd come together once before because it was right. How could coming together now be wrong? If anything, he wanted a chance to fix his mistake.

Something this good couldn't be bad.

Chapter 17

A T THE FIRST touch of his lips, the memories came flooding back. Lord, she wanted him. From that kiss, she hadn't been able to get enough. Eleven years hadn't changed that. But, now that the moment was upon them, she had no trouble stripping down to her skin and standing up as she always had. She went 100 percent into something; she didn't hold back. This was who she was.

When he'd followed suit, she couldn't resist. She'd gotten into his pants, and her hands had been all over him. It had always been like that. She could never stop touching him, stop kissing him.

They'd made love over and over again in that hotel room. So engrossed in each other, enjoying each other's passion so much that it had fueled their own, the night had been endless. When they had finally fallen asleep, it was as if somebody had hit them both with a reality checklist upon waking. It was shocking. They'd gone from hot to cold, and now all she could see was the heat burning through them again. And she wanted him. God, she wanted him even more.

And here she struggled to remain sane as those damn tantalizing fingers stroked and caressed her between her legs; his tongue tasted and dipped and curved and nibbled. She was already wet and open for him.

And yet he held back.

"No teasing," she ordered.

A slow sexy chuckle drifted up to her. She frowned. She knew that sound all too well. She sat up and grabbed him by the shoulders and tried to tug him toward her mouth. Instead, he dropped his head and kissed her right in the heart of the matter. She cried out, lifting her hips, instinctively seeking more.

He wrapped his hands around her hips and held her firm and resumed his torment. His tongue delved and tasted, and his hands wouldn't let her go.

By the time he finally moved to her hips, into her navel, and then to her breasts, she was mindless jelly. Once again she was so enthralled being with him that her mind no longer functioned as she went straight into fury—a conflagration that threatened to burn them both. She stroked and kissed and teased and bit him right back.

When he entered her, it was so right because her body was already his.

At his first plunge she screamed. At the second she screamed louder, and at the third she came apart.

Only he wasn't done. He held her locked in his arms and rode her through it and then reached down and found her tiny nub and teased her right into the second climax. And on it went.

When he finally collapsed beside her, she shook, her shivers literally wracking her body.

He could pull no blanket over them because he hadn't thought that far ahead.

Instead he covered her with his own body once again and whispered sweet nothings in her ear.

"Easy, baby. It's so damn beautiful to be with you again.

You're so passionate. So natural. So honest in your response. God, I love being here. How is it possible we walked away from this?"

He'd been like that. Not only did he wield his fingers and his hands and his mouth but his … voice. He always said the loveliest things to her. She felt cosseted. She felt adored. But most of all she felt loved. And that was the greatest feeling of all.

"Are you okay?" he asked in a low tone, his hand gently soothing up and down her shoulder.

"I will be," she whispered with a small laugh. "I forgot what it was like to make love with you."

He lowered his head and kissed her gently. "Hopefully it brought back just good memories."

She snaked her arms up around his neck and held him close. "The best."

He eased himself to the side and rolled her over so she was tucked against his chest. He slung a heavy leg over the top of hers and held her close. That was another thing she'd loved. After making love, he was the kind of guy who just held you close. Waited for the heartbeats to calm down and cuddled.

Every man should learn how to cuddle. She smiled at her thoughts and snuggled closer. "You were serious? Are we really getting to spend a week here doing this every night?"

She felt him startle, then the low, deep chuckle. Her smile widened. She tilted her head back slightly so she could look at his face. She batted her eyes at him and said, "Unless you had something else you want to do, like work or play cards."

He rolled her to her back once again, somehow landing between her spread legs. She could already feel the erection prodding her. "Already?"

And he slipped inside. "Already," he affirmed. "Besides, if we only have a week, we'd better make the most of it."

And they did.

That same night, they explored the upstairs and found several blankets, which they dragged back to the fireplace. With a bottle of wine they found in the cupboard, the night was endless. Of course by the time morning broke, they were so tired and dopey, the decision was to cuddle and just nap for the day.

And she loved it. She couldn't remember ever spending this much time in bed—except with Merk. The only two times it had happened, it had been with Merk. Well, no reason to rush away this time.

They moved upstairs later that day. Besides, the huge bed needed a christening.

Two days later, they slipped into a loverlike pattern of making love in the evening, making love in the morning, and then sure, why not make love in the afternoon? Because it all felt so damn good.

They were lost in a haze of romance she had never expected. No talk of their future, just lots of talk about their past, and who they were at this point in their lives.

On the third afternoon, while she cuddled with him on the couch, she said, "I don't know where to move. I don't think it's a good idea to stay in Houston."

"Where would you like to go?" He gently stroked a hand up and down her arm. "The world's a big place. Is there anywhere you want to go?"

She stared at him a moment. "Is it wrong to say, I want to be where you are?"

He gazed down at her with a smile in his eyes, making

her heart ache. She never expected to feel like this with anyone.

He gently stroked his thumb across her bottom lip. "But that would mean staying in Houston, or at least within an hour of that city."

She nodded. "I don't know if it would ever be safe for me."

"The company you worked for wasn't headquartered there. The business offices are in California, so chances are, by the time it's all shut down and cleaned out, it won't be an issue."

She liked the sound of that. Besides, it was a hell of a big city; the chances of ever meeting anybody she'd worked with were slim. And the ones she had worked with who were higher up would be, hopefully, going to jail.

Merk's phone rang just then. He shifted Katina to grab his cell from the side table. She lay on the couch, her head in his lap, and listened while he talked to Levi.

"No, no sign of anything here."

In her head she said, *Thankfully*. Because it had been idyllic, but she understood how something could interrupt their little vacation retreat anytime.

She waited for him to speak again. When she looked up, she could see a frown on his face and realized something wasn't good news. He shifted the phone so she could hear the conversation.

He smiled. "So they've picked up everyone but the big fish."

She waited breathlessly.

"And he was the one who had ordered Katina to be picked up. And had ordered the hit on Eloise. In other words, the one asshole we needed to catch is the one who's free. Shit." Silence again as Merk listened to Levi.

"Right, he's either on the run, or he's out picking off the witnesses who could put him away for life."

She listened, her heart getting heavy. Merk's tone of voice was harsh, and she realized this was probably the worst news ever.

The conversation continued but not a whole lot was different. When he got off the phone, the entire atmosphere changed. The side of Merk where she'd been resting her head was now locked down to hardened muscles.

"Are we leaving?" she asked quietly. Hating the idea but ready to go if necessary.

Immediately his hand came to rest on her shoulder. He then stroked the length of her arm and laced his fingers through hers. "No, not right now."

"So the main guy is still running around out there somewhere?"

He nodded. "And it's somebody who can identify you. Because it's your old boss. Robert Carlisle."

She bolted into a sitting position and twisted to look at him. "Robert?" At his nod she shook her head. "But he was a nice man. Why would he arrange a hit on me?"

He gave her a look that said, *You know why.*

She rolled her eyes back and said, "Okay, okay. I get why he did it. But he's the most normal-looking person you've ever met. He was nice. He always stopped and talked. He had time for everybody in the company."

"Chances were good he was just checking you were all following the company line and being good little robots," Merk said with a smile. "Do you know very much about him?"

"He loved to fish, and he had several favorite spots. His

family had a cabin on some lake. He often went there."

"And you know this how?"

"He used to bring back pictures of himself, holding up his trophies. On one trip, he came back with a particularly large fish, and he was so excited, he was telling everybody about where he got it."

"Do you happen to remember where?"

She frowned. "Something like Satsuma Lake or sounds like that." She shrugged. "Honestly, if he hadn't been my boss, I'd have turned and walked away. But, because of who he was, I stopped and smiled and made all the appropriate noises. But I really didn't give a damn because I can't stand fishing."

He gave her a look of horror. "You don't like to fish? That is every man's dream occupation."

She laughed. "And here I thought it was making love."

His grin flashed. "Okay, so fishing is a close second."

He opened his phone and called Levi back. "According to Katina, the man was an avid fisherman. And his family owns a cabin somewhere on a lake. Satsuma or something that sounds like that."

Katina reached across and grabbed his arm.

He raised an eyebrow. "Hang on, Levi. Katina has something else."

"In Samuel Cheevers wallet was an address—428 Morgan Street, Houston."

"Any idea what it means?"

She shook her head. "No, but it did say 11:00 p.m. beside it, so a meeting of some kind. But no date was given."

"Levi, did you hear that?" Merk hung up the phone and said, "Levi's checking it out."

"I really don't want to think about anyone still being out

there looking for me."

"It's all too possible. Which is why we never really can let our guard down. Until he's picked up, this isn't over."

THE NEXT DAY Merk answered the phone to hear the good news. He turned and beamed at Katina. "That was Levi. Apparently Robert was picked up at the cabin. As we suspected, he'd gone to ground. He didn't resist arrest—just came willingly. He's being booked downtown now."

She threw herself across him, screaming for joy.

He picked her up and turned her around. "Looks like we got this one beat. Cheevers isn't a threat any longer with all the bosses picked up. No incentive anymore for the low-level guys to keep on the job."

When he pulled back, he said, "Levi also said time to go home."

"Right now or tomorrow morning?" she asked with a leer.

He chuckled. "Considering it's only one o'clock in the afternoon, I would be hard pressed to come up with an excuse to not leave until tomorrow morning."

He watched her face fall, but she nodded. "I guess our holiday is over."

"Holiday? I thought we were building a relationship?"

She turned to look back at him in surprise, a smile dawning, slowly.

Breathtaking.

"We were too busy enjoying the moment," he said with a smile. "And you were talking about leaving. I didn't want to be the one who kept you from traveling, if that's what your heart desired."

She stepped into his arms and said, "Right now you're my heart's desire."

And she kissed him with those deep, slow, drugging kisses that she was so damn good at. His temperature was already peaking when she stepped back.

"Now we pack." With a laugh she left the room.

Damn. He sure wouldn't mind sticking around for a little longer. But Levi was right; it was time to get back to the real world.

He quickly emptied the fridge and cupboards. He pulled out Alfred's basket and loaded the remaining food in it.

As he put away the clean cups, he opened a different cupboard, his gaze, for the first time, going up to the second shelf, and he froze. His mind tried to not compute what his eyes saw, but it wasn't working. They'd been here, what, four days, and he hadn't noticed? Then again maybe it wasn't a listening device? He studied it, hoping for a different answer, but inside he knew exactly what it was.

In which case, if anybody was listening in, they would know exactly where Katina was. If it was one of Levi's devices, then no problem.

He considered the ramifications of that. Was it something Levi had in the house just in case? In which case, Merk hoped that his friends, for their sake, better not have been listening to the last three days of lovemaking. They'd have likely checked in, realized all was well, and checked out again. But what if that bug wasn't theirs? Others would know Katina was here. Except they'd been here for days already, and nobody had come. He leaned back against the counter as he pulled out his phone and called Levi.

He could hear the puzzlement in Levi's voice as he said, "I don't think we have a bug there."

Merk stood and waited, the bug in his hand, as Levi turned from the phone and asked Ice.

Merk could hear the muffled response as Ice said, "No."

"Okay. Any idea why nobody has come then?"

"The good answer would be because we've picked up all the perps who were listening or monitoring the situation. The bad answer would be they've decided attacking you in the house was no good, so they're waiting for you to make a move."

Shit. He ended the call as a second one came through immediately. He answered it, his gaze locked on the listening device. But his mind was on Levi's information. "Hello."

"Get out. Now. Drop everything and go." His brother, Terkel's, voice was hard and sure. "Don't argue. This is good-as-dead bad. Move your ass now."

Ah, hell. "Time frame?"

"You've got five minutes. In ten it's too late."

And in typical Terkel fashion, he was gone. But Merk could hear his brother's whispered voice in the back of his head, ending with the phrase he always did, *Good luck, brother.*

They had to move ... and now. His brother was never wrong.

Yet someone was out there lying in wait. Someone already on the move.

Chapter 18

GOING HOME WAS supposed be the easy part. But she knew nothing would be easy about it when Merk disappeared outside, telling her to stay inside and pack fast, he'd be back in two minutes, and they needed to go immediately afterward.

She bit down on her bottom lip to stop herself from protesting. She had to trust he knew what he was doing. If it was just cautionary measures, it was all good. But based on his words and tone, it was something so much worse. With her bags packed and sitting beside the door, she quickly made a pot of coffee while she waited. Then proceeded to fill two thermoses.

After cleaning up, she still had no sign of Merk. She made another round to check they had packed everything and deliberately left the fridge open and turned off. She didn't know if somebody would be in to clean the cabin, but, as it was empty, it seemed wasteful to leave the fridge running. Who knew how long it would be until someone else stayed here. She hated this dithering. Making a decision, then changing her mind, not knowing what to do. Finally she sat down on top of her bag at the back door and waited.

Until she heard unfamiliar footsteps on the porch ...

She froze.

From where she sat, she couldn't see who it was. She

didn't want to move in case it alerted whoever was there that she was inside. She cast her mind back to the last few minutes, wondering if she'd been in front of the windows and if somebody could have seen her.

When she heard no sound of Merk entering the house or calling her name, her nerves set in. Followed immediately by panic. She glanced at the back door she sat beside and realized it wasn't even locked.

The footstep she'd heard were on the other side of the porch. She didn't know if they were coming toward her or not. If she locked the door now, they'd know she was here. But, if she left it unlocked, they'd get in easily. It probably made no difference because none of these walls or windows would keep them outside anyway. If he wanted in, he would get in. Her only hope was that Merk had seen him and was even now hunting down the asshole.

She whispered a prayer in her mind, *Please let this be Merk.*

She waited, her jaw clenched, her arms wrapped around her chest. And again she heard nothing. She was just about to convince herself she hadn't heard a footstep, maybe just a branch cracking outside instead. She was being foolish ... when the doorknob in front of her moved ever-so-slightly.

She bounded to her feet, snapped the bolt down, and raced for the front door. She was outside, into the woods in seconds. She didn't stop running until she was in the middle of a thick stand of evergreens. She hadn't seen or heard anyone running after her, but that didn't ease her panic.

Catching sight of one big evergreen, she bolted for the low branches and climbed up. She didn't stop until she was buried in the upper branches and completely hidden from view.

In her mind she knew that couldn't have been Merk. He would have said something. No way he'd have terrorized her like that. And that meant somebody else was here.

Still not feeling safe at the level she'd attained, she crept up higher. She clung to the tree trunk, buried deep in the branches. She realized her jacket was a light blue and could be spotted easily. Her black T-shirt was on underneath. Stripping off the jacket, she stuffed it between her and the tree trunk.

She didn't know how long it would be before she was found, but no way in hell was she moving until she knew Merk was below her. Katina couldn't hear anything because her heart slamming against her ribs drowned out everything else. She worked at getting a deep breath out and then another one. Anything to prevent that panic attack from taking over. She'd never had one, but this was a justifiable time.

When she didn't hear anything for what felt like ten minutes, her breathing slowed to a more normal rate. By the time probably twenty minutes had lapsed, she peered through the boughs to see if anybody was around. After what had to have been a full half hour gone by, she wondered whether she'd been an idiot and had run for nothing.

But Merk wasn't back here with her.

And no way could she have misinterpreted that doorknob turning.

When she crossed what surely had been the forty-five-minute mark, she reassessed the branch she was on, wondering if another would allow her to rest her back or to sit down better. She still had no intention of climbing down, but, for the first time, reality set in.

Horrible thoughts crossed her mind. What if the intruder had taken Merk out already? Then, it would be just her and the bad guy. Hell, if he'd seen her come in this direction, he could just sit on the front step and wait for her. She'd have to get down sometime. She hadn't planned on this being an all-night thing. She should've found a place inside the house to hide. At least then, when he left, she would have supplies.

But her brain immediately kicked in and said, *To last until when?* Until he came back? And why would he leave at all? She felt in her pockets and smiled. Instantly she kicked herself for being such a fool. She had her phone on her. She pulled it out, turned off the sound so nobody could hear calls incoming and outgoing, and texted Merk.

Where are you?

The answer came back instantly.

Stay where you are.

At least he'd answered. So he was alive. And obviously hunting the intruder. He'd told her to stay inside the house, but what was she supposed to do when the intruder was coming inside via the back door?

Unless he'd planned on taking the guy out at the house. But killing herself with all those self-doubts wasn't helping. At the same time she didn't know if Levi had any idea what was going on. She wondered if she should tell him. Just in case things got ugly.

The thing was, if it went bad, she needed somebody to know where she was, and, if things went good, well, that meant she was looking out for Merk and reporting in. Which made it an easy decision for her.

She opened the phone, thankful she'd been given everybody's number at the compound. She didn't know if that was a sign of trust or if they just still considered her part of the problem. She appreciated it either way. She immediately fired off texts to Levi and Ice. She wasn't sure who else would be around but figured Stone might be and sent him one too.

The responses came back instantly.

Don't move.

Stay where you are.

Trust Merk. Listen to him.

She stared down at the short answers and shook her head. *Really? That's it? I'm supposed to sit in this tree and just wait?*

Still, the advice wasn't bad. She studied the few branches around her and realized she could carefully lower herself to straddle the branch she stood on, allowing her to lean back against the trunk. But she had to do it so the tree didn't move; otherwise somebody might notice where she was. And, although the intruder might know Merk was here, the intruder's end result was going after her. She was the target. Besides, she figured these guys were arrogant enough to think they could handle Merk. Idiots.

Moving carefully she finally settled on the branch in a more relaxed position. Waiting had never been her thing, but, given her options, she figured she could stay here and do as she was told. As she sat and thought about all that she and Merk had, and the future that lay before them, she got angry.

Because this asshole could destroy her chances at that future. She understood the last few days with Merk had been a fantasy bubble of sexy romance, but they'd needed that time. No way would she let the asshole destroy what she and Merk had forged together.

She reconsidered her options. They all sucked. She had no weapon. If she did have one, she wouldn't know how to use it. Merk was well-trained and was out there, knowing exactly what was going on and how to handle this asshole.

Just then she heard something that made all the logic in the world disappear in a flash.

Gunfire filled the air. Silence, then more shots cracked.

Instantly she went into panic mode, pulling her knees up against her chest, making herself into as small a ball as she possibly could. She held her breath, waiting for the dust to settle. Who had gotten shot? And the bigger question still in her mind was, is Merk okay? She snatched up her phone and texted the others to say **Gunfire**. She texted Merk next.

Are you okay?

His answer was short.

Yes. Don't move.

And she realized the fight was still not over. She bowed her head and swore she would never get involved in something like this again.

HOPEFULLY SHE'D LISTEN this time. He peered around the trees. He understood why she'd bolted from the guy trying to get into the house. And he'd seen her mad dash into the woods and figured she got up a tree. If she'd just damn well stay there until he took down this asshole, they'd be good.

This guy needed to be taken out so they didn't have to look over their shoulders anymore. Likely a contract killer, one asshole determined to finish the job. Merk had missed him at the house. He'd run around the deck and gone after her, but she'd run like a rabbit. Something Merk had been happy to see. He knew exactly how fit and in shape she was. Because he'd spent a lot of hours stroking those toned muscles. But she still couldn't outrun a bullet.

His gaze swept the stands of trees yet again.

Crack.

He instantly dropped to the ground.

A bullet slammed into the tree trunk where he'd been standing. Damn it. The asshole had somehow circled around and come up behind him. The game of hide-and-seek was on.

Merk pulled himself up on several limbs of the tree to get better visibility. He caught sight of movement on the left. He turned and let his gaze float across the area, still just waiting to see ... anything. A small shrub shivered with movement from within.

He lined up the shot. The brush was a good thirty-five yards away. Depending on how many branches were in the way, he had a good chance of hitting him.

He took the shot.

A man grunted. Even that much sound echoed loudly in the silent woods. He might have hit him, but he couldn't tell for sure.

Sighting his target, he slipped off to the right and kept moving to higher ground. He wanted to come down from behind. As he watched, the gunman straightened, turned, and stared right at him, but his gaze drifted off to the side.

He hadn't seen Merk.

Perfect. Merk straightened up ever-so-slightly and fired. The only sound was a soft thud. Keeping behind the tree trunks, he raced toward his victim. And, sure enough, he'd shot him in the neck. The man was dead.

Kicking away the man's weapon just in case, he bent down and pulled out his wallet to check his ID. But when he read John Lennon with an address in Washington, he figured it was fake. He straightened up, intent on picking up the guy and carrying him around to the front of the cabin when he heard something that made his heart run cold.

And realized he'd been a fool. The dead man hadn't been alone.

"Just drop him. He was an idiot anyway."

Merk raised his hands and slowly turned to face his newest adversary. Merk didn't know him, but he obviously was a better professional than the one on the ground.

The man grinned and said, "Young trainees make great decoys. It's amazing how often you guys, who think you're so damn good, find out how dead wrong you are."

"That's because he's the only one who did any of the shooting," Merk said calmly. His mind raced, looking for opportunities—they were looking pretty damn shitty. Plus he had to keep in mind this guy was after Katina. Even if Merk took a bullet, that wouldn't end this. He had to take down this asshole too. Otherwise he'd go after Katina.

And that wasn't going to happen.

"Well, it's nice to know you can tell the difference between the guns." He motioned with the barrel of his. "Turn around." When Merk complied, he added, "Now walk over to your girlfriend. See if she'll come down from that tree on her own."

His heart sank. He walked a few steps and said, "You

know you won't get away with this."

The man behind him laughed. "Of course I will. Do you have any idea how many other missions like this I've completed?"

"Missions?" Interesting phrase. So he was military too. "You didn't like the military and moved into the private sector? Private contracts?"

"Yep, much better pay. The benefits are nicer too."

Merk nodded in friendly acknowledgment as he continued to walk closer to Katina's hiding place. "Just out of curiosity, what happens to your contract now that your boss has been picked up?"

"I've already been paid. Completing the job is a matter of pride. A contract can't go unfinished, as my word is everything."

Merk understood. It also meant it didn't matter that the DA had rounded everyone up and was even now preparing for the court case. If the DA wanted Katina as a witness, then having her go missing would weaken the case. So the men in jail were counting on the assassin to complete the job. "Too bad. I was hoping maybe you'd drop the contract when you realized it was over already."

"Not happening. I don't care how many of these assholes the law picks up. I hope the jailers throw away the keys. They aren't men I want in this world if they think killing a woman because she saw something is the way to handle their problems. If they'd hung on to her after the kidnapping instead of letting her escape, they'd not need me. But they are all idiots."

Merk changed direction slightly, heading away from Katina, only to get slugged in the head.

"Don't bother. You and I both know where she is hiding."

Merk turned slightly and headed back in her direction. He needed a diversion. Something to allow him to tackle this asshole. He might be military, ex-military, but so was Merk, so he'd be using his dirtiest techniques.

"Stop here."

And that just confirmed what Merk had suspected. They were literally below the tree where Katina was hiding.

"Call her down."

He hesitated, wondering at the sense of doing that. But he called out, "Katina, run when you can."

And he dropped to the ground and kicked the man's legs out from under him. The gunman was on Merk in an instant. The gun went flying, and it was down to fists and as many underhanded tactics as they could use. The fight was vicious. Both knowing, in the end, one was going down.

Each needed to be the victor. Merk had more to lose. He had Katina.

He punched, kicked, flipped, and took several blows to the face—delivering twice as many as he got—but he could never quite get ahead.

The other man swore, then cried out, "You son of a bit—"

A puzzled look came into the killer's eyes before they rolled up into the back of his head. And he collapsed on top of Merk.

Merk shoved him off and bounced to his feet. Katina stood in front of him. He turned to look down at the killer to see a thick stick, one end thinner than the other sticking out of his back.

Instantly he opened his arms, and she ran into them. He crushed her against his chest, realizing how close he'd come to losing her.

When he finally eased his grip on her, she stepped aside, swung her hand back, and smacked him across the face. Pissed, he yelled, "What the hell was that for?"

"For suggesting I run away and leave you to deal with him on your own." She fisted her hands on her hips and glared at him. "Did you really expect me to save myself and forget about you? We're in this together—remember?"

Shocked, he stared at her, then glanced down at the dead man on the ground and started to laugh. He opened his arms again, and she fell into them, hugging him tight.

"Together? As in together forever?" She tilted her head and stared at him with the question in her eyes.

"Are you asking me this time?" he said with a laugh.

As she sputtered, he lowered his head and kissed her. When he stopped, this time she looked up at him with tear-laced eyes and whispered, "I thought I'd lost you again."

"I'm not so easy to lose," he said with a smile. He wrapped his arm around her shoulders and led her back to the cabin. "We'll stay here a little longer to deal with the bodies."

At the surprised look on her face, he realized she didn't know about the first man. He explained, watching the color leech from her face.

She swallowed hard and asked, "Then can we go home?"

"Absolutely."

As they reached the cabin, his phone rang. He glanced down to see Levi's number.

That's when she said apologetically, "I contacted them when I was in the tree."

He rolled his eyes and answered the call. "Yes, Levi. I'm fine, and so is she. It's over, but we have two bodies here to be picked up."

He listened as Levi, all business, made plans and filled him in on the latest. "Samuel Cheevers was picked up alive and well at the Morgan address, so good job on that," Levi said. "I have someone on the way for the latest two you've taken out."

Merk snorted at that. "Not my fault. But we're here until law enforcement gets here."

"And then where are you going?" Levi asked curiously. "Are you coming back here or … are you heading to Vegas?" he finished drily.

"I don't think so. At least not right away," Merk joked. He rang off and put away his phone.

At the silence at his side, he turned toward Katina to tell her of the plans in motion, only to frown at the look on her face. "What's the matter?"

"Was it a mistake?" she asked softly.

He didn't know exactly what she was referring too and knew it was a pathway riddled with mines if he didn't navigate this safety.

"Was what a mistake?" he asked cautiously, feeling his way.

"Marrying me?"

His gaze widened. "Hell, no. As a matter of fact, I was thinking we needed to repeat it as soon as possible."

She narrowed her gaze at him.

He tilted her chin up and kissed her, then, with his lips quirking into a lopsided smile, he said, "We could make a fast trip to Vegas."

She snickered. "I will *not* get married for a second time in the Elvis Presley Wedding Chapel," she stated firmly.

"That's okay. How about a Dracula's Tomb wedding?

I'm sure that would be a scream," he said jokingly.

But her response surprised him. She threw her arms around his neck and said, "I love you. Might always have loved you, but no way in hell am I going back to Vegas to get married again."

He wrapped his arms around her and held her close.

"But ..." she added, her breath warm against his lips, "any other place in the world—I'm all for it."

He didn't dare tell her there were some pretty godawful venues in Reno too. He figured he'd leave that for another time.

He was partial to a Dracula's Tomb wedding himself.

Maybe if he gave her some time to consider it ...

Then he caught sight of her face and realized it wouldn't matter where the ceremony took place—as long as she became his wife again—so all was good.

Epilogue

R HODES WALKED IN with another armload of groceries. The compound had been flying high these last few days. The DA was particularly impressed with the job Levi and the team had done in protecting Katina and helping to bring a lot of serious badasses to justice. Of course the court system was long and arduous with no guarantee of a conviction, but the DA had said, with the amount of information everyone had collected, it should be an easy run.

After Rhodes dropped the box of groceries on the kitchen counter for Alfred, he walked back out to grab yet another one. He smiled at Katina and Merk, standing in a clench off to the side. As he walked past, in a loud voice he said, "Unless you're making wedding chapel suggestions, I suggest you two come and help unload the truck."

Katina pulled back, laughing. "Sorry, Rhodes. Every time I get close to this guy, it's like a magnet pulling me in."

"And that's the way it should be," Sienna said loyally from behind Rhodes.

Rhodes wanted to say something, but Sienna was a best friend's sister, and, as such, he was still treating her with kid gloves as he had done when she'd been a gawky teenager with stunning promise. Unfortunately that was the last thing he wanted to do with her now.

It sucked when all your buddies were pairing up, and

you were the one left out. Especially when the one you wanted was out of bounds.

Her brother, Jarrod, had been to the compound twice already and was due for a third visit later today, all to ensure his sister was truly all right, especially now that the place had calmed down somewhat after the two recent attacks here at the compound, plus Jarrod had been called on a second overseas mission. Rhodes planned to talk to Jarrod as soon as he got here.

Sienna might not know what she had gotten herself into by asking for a permanent job at Legendary Security, but she'd better stick around now because he had no intention of letting this one go—ever.

Rhodes just hoped his SEAL-brother Jarrod thought that was a good idea too.

This concludes Book 3 of Heroes for Hire: Merk's Mistake.

Book 4 is available.

Rhodes' Reward: Heroes for Hire, Book 4

Buy this book at your favorite vendor.

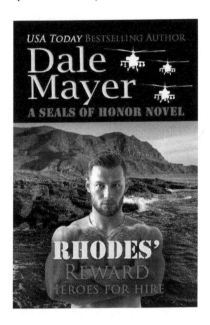

Welcome *to Rhodes' Reward*, book 4 in Heroes for Hire, reconnecting readers with the unforgettable men from SEALs of Honor in a new series of action packed, page turning romantic suspense that fans have come to expect from USA TODAY Bestselling author Dale Mayer.

Second chances do happen... Even amid evil...

Rhodes knew Sienna years ago. When she'd been young and gawky, more elbow and carrot hair than style, but she'd had something special even then. Now she's all grown. But she's a trouble magnet, and even at the compound it finds her…

Sienna had a super-sized crush on her brother's best friend years ago. Now he's hunky and even hotter than she could have imagined. Only she's new and doesn't want to jeopardize her position. When asked to help out on a job, she agrees…and triggers a sequence of disastrous events no one could foresee.

But someone will stop at nothing to silence everyone involved, especially the two of them…

Heroes for Hire Series

Author's Note

Thanks for reading. By now many of you have read my explanation of how I love to see **Star Ratings.** The only catch is that we as authors have no idea what you think of a book if it's not reviewed. And yes, **every book in a series needs reviews.** All it takes is a little as two words: Fun Story. Yep, that's all. So, if you enjoyed reading, please take a second to let others know you enjoyed.

For those of you who have not read a previous book and have no idea why we authors keep asking you as a reader to take a few minutes to leave even a two word review, here's more explanation of reviews in this crazy business.

Reviews (not just ratings) help authors qualify for advertising opportunities and help other readers make purchasing decisions. Without *triple digit* reviews, an author may miss out on valuable advertising opportunities. And with only "star ratings" the author has little chance of participating in certain promotions. Which means fewer sales offered to my favorite readers!

Another reason to take a minute and leave a review is that often a **few kind words left in a review can make a huge difference to an author and their muse.** Recently new to reviewing fans have left a few words after reading a similar letter and they were tonic to tired muse! LOL Seriously. Star ratings simply do not have the same impact to thank or encourage an author when the writing gets tough.

So please consider taking a moment to write even a handful of words. Writing a review only takes a few minutes of your time. It doesn't have to be a lengthy book report, just a few words expressing what you enjoyed most about the story. Here are a few tips of how to leave a review.

Please continue to rate the books as you read, but take an extra moment and pop over to the review section and leave a few words too!

Most of all – **Thank you** for reading. I look forward to hearing from you.

I love to hear from readers, and you can contact me at my website: www.dalemayer.com or at my Facebook author page. To be informed of new releases and special offers, sign up for my newsletter. And if you are interested in joining Dale Mayer's Fan Club, here is the Facebook sign up page. facebook.com/groups/402384989872660

Cheers,
Dale Mayer

COMPLIMENTARY DOWNLOAD

DOWNLOAD a *__complimentary__* copy of TUESDAY'S CHILD? Just tell me where to send it!

http://dalemayer.com/starterlibrarytc/

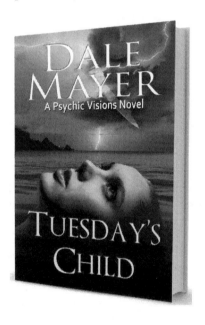

Touched by Death

Adult RS/thriller

Get this book at your favorite vendor.

Death had touched anthropologist Jade Hansen in Haiti once before, costing her an unborn child and perhaps her very sanity.

A year later, determined to face her own issues, she returns to Haiti with a mortuary team to recover the bodies of an American family from a mass grave. Visiting his brother after the quake, independent contractor Dane Carter puts his life on hold to help the sleepy town of Jacmel rebuild. But he finds it hard to like his brother's pregnant wife or her family. He wants to go home, until he meets Jade – and realizes what's missing in his own life. When the mortuary team begins work, it's as if malevolence has been released from the earth. Instead of laying her ghosts to rest, Jade finds herself confronting death and terror again.

And the man who unexpectedly awakens her heart – is right in the middle of it all.

By Death Series

Touched by Death – Part 1

Touched by Death – Part 2

Touched by Death – Parts 1&2

Haunted by Death

Chilled by Death

By Death Books 1–3

Vampire in Denial
This is book 1 of the Family Blood Ties Saga

Get this book at your favorite vendor.

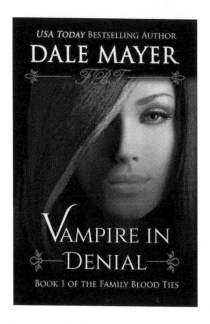

Blood doesn't just make her who she is...it also makes her what she is.

Like being a sixteen-year-old vampire isn't hard enough, Tessa's throwback human genes make her an outcast among her relatives. But try as she might, she can't get a handle on the vampire lifestyle and all the...blood.

Turning her back on the vamp world, she embraces the human teenage lifestyle—high school, peer pressure and finding a boyfriend. Jared manages to stir something in her blood. He's smart and fun and oh, so cute. But Tessa's dream of a having the perfect boyfriend turns into a nightmare when vampires attack the movie theatre and kidnap her date.

Once again, Tessa finds herself torn between the human world and the vampire one. Will blood own out? Can she make peace with who she is as well as what?

Warning: This book ends with a cliffhanger! Book 2 picks up where this book ends.

Family Blood Ties Series

Vampire in Denial

Vampire in Distress

Vampire in Design

Vampire in Deceit

Vampire in Defiance

Vampire in Conflict

Vampire in Chaos

Vampire in Crisis

Vampire in Control

Vampire in Charge

Family Blood Ties Set 1–3

Family Blood Ties Set 1–5

Family Blood Ties Set 4–6

Family Blood Ties Set 7–9

Sian's Solution – A Family Blood Ties Short Story

Broken Protocols

Get this book at your favorite vendor.

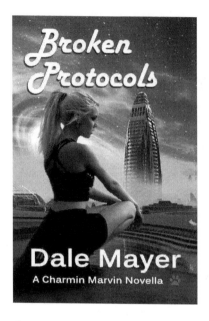

Dani's been through a year of hell...

Just as it's getting better, she's tossed forward through time with her orange Persian cat, Charmin Marvin, clutched in her arms. They're dropped into a few centuries into the future. There's nothing she can do to stop it, and it's impossible to go back.

And then it gets worse...

A year of government regulation is easing, and Levi Blackburn is feeling back in control. If he can keep his reckless brother in check, everything will be perfect. But while he's been protecting Milo from the government, Milo's been busy working on a present for him...

The present is Dani, only she comes with a snarky cat who suddenly starts talking...and doesn't know when to shut up.

In an age where breaking protocols have severe consequences, things go wrong, putting them all in danger...

Charmin Marvin Romantic Comedy Series

About the Author

Dale Mayer is a USA Today bestselling author best known for her Psychic Visions and Family Blood Ties series. Her contemporary romances are raw and full of passion and emotion (Second Chances, SKIN), her thrillers will keep you guessing (By Death series), and her romantic comedies will keep you giggling (It's a Dog's Life and Charmin Marvin Romantic Comedy series).

She honors the stories that come to her – and some of them are crazy and break all the rules and cross multiple genres!

To go with her fiction, she also writes nonfiction in many different fields with books available on resume writing, companion gardening and the US mortgage system. She has recently published her Career Essentials Series. All her books are available in print and ebook format.

Connect with Dale Mayer Online

Dale's Website – www.dalemayer.com
Twitter – @DaleMayer
Facebook – facebook.com/DaleMayer.author

Also by Dale Mayer

Published Adult Books:

Psychic Vision Series

Tuesday's Child

Hide'n Go Seek

Maddy's Floor

Garden of Sorrow

Knock, Knock...

Rare Find

Eyes to the Soul

Now You See Her

Shattered

Into the Abyss

Seeds of Malice

Eye of the Falcon

Psychic Visions Books 1–3

Psychic Visions Books 4–6

Psychic Visions Books 7–9

By Death Series

Touched by Death – Part 1

Touched by Death – Part 2

Touched by Death – Parts 1&2

Haunted by Death

Chilled by Death

By Death Books 1–3

Second Chances...at Love Series

Second Chances – Part 1

Second Chances – Part 2

Second Chances – complete book (Parts 1 & 2)

Charmin Marvin Romantic Comedy Series

Broken Protocols

Broken Protocols 2

Broken Protocols 3

Broken Protocols 3.5

Broken Protocols 1-3

Broken and... Mending

Skin

Scars

Scales (of Justice)

Broken but... Mending 1-3

Glory

Genesis

Tori

Celeste

Glory Trilogy

Biker Blues

Biker Blues: Morgan, Part 1

SEALs of Honor

Heroes for Hire

Merk's Mistake: Heroes for Hire, Book 3

Rhodes' Reward: Heroes for Hire, Book 4

Flynn's Firecracker: Heroes for Hire, Book 5

Logan's Light: Heroes for Hire, Book 6

Harrison's Heart: Heroes for Hire, Book 7

Jarrod's Jewel: Heroes for Hire, Book 8

Collections

Dare to Be You...

Dare to Love...

Dare to be Strong...

RomanceX3

Standalone Novellas

It's a Dog's Life

Riana's Revenge

Published Young Adult Books:

Family Blood Ties Series

Vampire in Denial

Vampire in Distress

Vampire in Design

Vampire in Deceit

Vampire in Defiance

Vampire in Conflict

Vampire in Chaos

Vampire in Crisis

Vampire in Control

Vampire in Charge

Family Blood Ties Set 1–3
Family Blood Ties Set 1–5
Family Blood Ties Set 4–6
Family Blood Ties Set 7–9
Sian's Solution – A Family Blood Ties Short Story

Design series
Dangerous Designs
Deadly Designs
Darkest Designs
Design Series Trilogy

Standalone
In Cassie's Corner
Gem Stone (a Gemma Stone Mystery)
Time Thieves

Published Non-Fiction Books:

Career Essentials
Career Essentials: The Résumé
Career Essentials: The Cover Letter
Career Essentials: The Interview
Career Essentials: 3 in 1

70735011R00125

Made in the USA
Lexington, KY
15 November 2017